BEATING THE DEVIL

Beating the DEVIL

W. C. JAMESON

University of New Mexico Press
ALBUQUERQUE

Printed in the United States of America

12 11 10 09 08 07 1 2 3 4 5 6 7

Library of Congress Cataloging-in-Publication Data

Jameson, W. C., 1942–
Beating the devil / W.C. Jameson.
p. cm.
ISBN 978-0-8263-4039-9 (alk. paper)
1. Americans—Mexico—Fiction. 2. Mexico—Fiction.
3. Nineteen twenties—Fiction. 4. Nineteen thirties—Fiction.
I. Title.
PS3610.A467B43 2007
813'.6—dc22
2007009888

Book design and composition by Damien Shay
Body type is Utopia 10/14
Display is Rumpled Roman

For

Laurie Wagner Buyer

Luz de mi vida,

who peeled back the layers

and the years

and pulled this story

out of the darkness

and into the light

There is no God in Mexico.
That is why we spend so much
of our time beating back the devil.

—Old man on the plaza,
Ciudad Chihuahua,
August 1961

Pity poor Mexico: So far from God,
so close to the United States.

—Porfirio Díaz,
former president of Mexico

The Dreams

Los Sueños

The dreams come on moonless nights when the light of the sun shines on another part of the world. They engulf me, overwhelm me, until I am left panting and sweating, screaming, begging for my life. They surface, malevolent serpents out of black water. When they rise, I tremble, vibrating with such intensity I fear I will shatter. I am afraid to remain in bed, afraid that if I do I will be unable to keep the dreams at bay. Weak and exhausted, I hesitate. I cannot rise to search for the light. Nor do I wish to, for I fear that the dreams will not vanish, that they have become real.

When the dreams come I taste the dust, the dry, swirling Mexican earth kicked up by galloping horses and running men. I smell sweat and blood—the pervasive, coppery, throat-constricting odor of blood. I hear gunshots, shouting, cursing. In my dreams I hear the sound of blood of other men, blood that has been released from its passageways by bullets and knives and, unrestricted, explodes into the air turning from black to red. I see color, a sharp crimson seeping into my white cotton shirt, spreading outward.

In the dreams, I hear mourners weeping, men praying, babies crying, and the sound of church bells tolling in the distance in a faraway land. In the dreams there are battlegrounds of red, brown, and yellow earth, of dust and smoke, that dissolve slowly to scenes of verdant bottomlands where mockingbirds and sparrows sing from the cottonwoods and narrow streams and acequias filled with cool, clear water wind across flat green fields.

People with skin the color of the soil and rock and smoke beckon me, entreat me to return. I wake shaking, with saline streams dried upon my face.

There are nights when I dread going to bed, when I am terrified of sleep. When I finally succumb, the dreams come to me, wrap me in layers of sound, color, smell, texture. I fear the dreams, but I also long for them. I embrace them.

The dreams and I are the same.

For forty years I kept the secret that fueled the dreams hidden in a light cardboard box, the kind in which a ream of typing paper is sold, all packed away under the accumulated debris of living.

One afternoon thirty-five years after my return from Mexico in 1931, I found the box while moving some items out of a storage shed. Lying under heavier boxes, it was crushed, the corners torn and ragged. With a palpable aura of uncertainty and no little trepidation, I ceased my chore and carried the box to my study, sat at my writing desk, and placed it on my lap, tense, apprehensive. With caution, as if in fear of releasing a monster, I removed the lid and stared at the loose, scattered contents: some sixty poems handwritten on hotel stationery, notebook paper, lunch bags, the backs of used envelopes, canceled checks, paper napkins, and even on the blank margins of newspaper pages.

Memories, rising out of the box like wisps of smoke, curled around me, blurring my vision, tightening my chest, pulling me back to that long-ago time and place. The recollections, unbidden, charged me like careering horses. When I couldn't get out of the way, they ran me down, trampling me into the dust of the past, into unconsciousness.

An hour later, when I returned to full awareness, I was lying on the floor, the open box of poems clutched tightly in my hands, my shirt drenched in sweat. I struggled to sit up, and unable to stop the tears, I cried until I was dry.

I knew then that I had to tell this story. It has not been easy. I am the only one left; the others are all dead.

The Crossing

El Cruce

My mother told me never to go to the river crossing. She said it was a bad place, an evil place. Men had been killed at the crossing, she said. Children had disappeared at the crossing, and she insisted they were carried deep into Mexico, into the Sierra Madres, and put to work in the mines and fields where they were beaten and starved and not permitted to pray. Praying was important to my mother. She told me many stories about women who were caught harvesting wild asparagus along the riverbank near the crossing and endured the unspeakable. Their families and friends shunned them forever thereafter.

My mother once said, "Carlos, the river will steal your soul and you will be doomed to wander forever without God."

My mother told me to stay away from Old Simon who spent his days walking along the riverbank near the crossing. She said he was dirty, an Indian, that he was a drunk and an evil man. Old Simon told me it was sad that my mother was trying to raise three children alone.

Old Simon told me the crossing was a haunted place. He also said it was seductive, the cool shade of the nearby large cottonwood an oft-sought haven from the burning West Texas sun. Old Simon was half Yaqui Indian and half Irish, and he lived in a sheet metal, scrap wood, and cardboard hovel at the edge of a cotton field not far from the crossing. Old Simon had crossed the river into Mexico many times, he said. For days, weeks, he disappeared into the interior, into the tall mountains and the dark canyons of the Sierra Madres. No one knew where he went or what he did. Old Simon, with his Indian-cast complexion and black hair and dark eyes, was more at home in a Mexican pueblo than the towns of Texas.

Stories were told that Old Simon had been a bandit in Mexico, that he robbed travelers and stores and trains, that he had killed men. It was whispered that he harvested the wild peyote from the Sierra del Carmens in Coahuila and brought it back to sell to *los indios* along the border near Laredo and Del Río. These stories didn't make sense to me: why would Old Simon live in a run-down, leaky shack if he possessed the wealth from robberies and selling peyote?

Old Simon told me stories about the crossing. He said at least a dozen men had been hung from the limbs of the *álamo grande*, the great, thick cottonwood tree that grew near the bank of the river next to the crossing where the goats came to feed. Old Simon said the soil beneath the álamo was stained red from the blood of men who had been shot and killed there.

Old Simon told me the crossing was just a few yards upstream from the álamo grande. It was a flat, narrow underwater bar of coarse river gravel that had been used for centuries, first by the Apaches and Comanches, later by the Spanish explorers, and still later by horse and cattle thieves moving stock across the border. Now, he said, it was mostly used by the *mojados*—wetbacks—making their way into Texas. The Mexicans knew of the crossing, he said, because its location had been passed down from father to son for untold generations. On the upstream and downstream sides of the crossing, Old Simon warned, the river sands were soft and yielding, and anyone or anything stepping from the underwater bridge would sink into the quicksand and never be seen again. He told of cattle and horses and men that had been caught by the loose, saturated sands, sank out of sight within minutes.

The Río Grande flowed only three hundred yards from our low, flat-roofed, native sandstone house. A trail leading to it ran from the backyard of the casa across a drainage ditch, through a canebrake, an abandoned cotton field, and to the terrace overlooking the floodplain of the river.

I was eleven years old when I first came to the crossing. It was on a day when my mother, in her gardenia-patterned housedress and worn, oft-repaired shoes, took her long walk down the dirt road to buy a few groceries. She walked purposefully, clutching her thread-bare canvas purse containing a few bills and coins. My seven-year-old sister and three-year-old brother followed, stopping now and then to play in the pockets of gravel and search for attractive stones.

I watched from the front window, and when they rounded a curve and were out of sight, I dashed out the back door and ran toward the path that led to the crossing. Trailing at my heels was my dog Pete. Pete was half-Chihuahua and half-unknown but would take on larger dogs while defending me. He had been my close companion for six years.

I passed a copse of stunted river oaks and came to the edge of the terrace that overlooked the river and the floodplain. Near the bank of the Río Grande, stretching dozens of feet upward and outward, was the álamo grande, its bole as thick as a cluster of half a dozen men, its leafy branches shading the sand beneath. I imagined men hanging by their necks from the thick limbs, their limp bodies swinging in the unceasing West Texas wind. Just beyond, the brown, muddy river flowed languidly, inviting.

I walked over to the tree and stood in the cool shade. I touched the rough bark, running my fingers across the corrugated husk. I searched the soil at my feet for bloodstains. I stared at the river flowing gulfward. Pete stood next to me, eyeing an approaching herd of goats.

On the opposite side of the river another floodplain, a twin to the one on which I stood, stretched southward toward a distant counterpart terrace edged with a line of álamos. The cottonwoods barely concealed a small pueblo about a quarter of a mile further, home to perhaps two hundred. I could just make out the squat adobe houses in the distance. I could hear the faint muffled voices of *la gente* (the people), voices carried by the wind. Dust, kicked up by the eddying air, flowed from adjacent fields.

Dominating the village was a missionlike stone and stucco structure that rose above the one-story casas and *tiendas*. Silhouetted just above the line of trees was a tall cross mounted on the roof-swell of the church. In the afternoon light, the cross reflected a crimson hue that contrasted with the dirt-colored adobe and rock buildings of the pueblo. I stared at the cross until it grew apart from the village and seemed to take on a life of its own. It hovered in the air like *el zopilote*, the vulture.

A pair of goats pushed into the ring of shade from the álamo and butted against my thighs. I glanced up and spotted an old man several yards away who was watching me. He was wearing baggy cotton *pantalones* common to the campesinos, a worn serape, and a battered straw sombrero. The goatherd nodded, and with a slight wave of his arm, ambled on, turning his attention back to the herd grazing on the rich grasses of the floodplain.

I stared again at the river and the land beyond. I looked to the west. The sun had sunk to the top of the ridge of the mountains beyond Ciudad Juárez. Low, blood red, it stretched the shadow of the álamo dozens of yards eastward along the plain paralleling the river. A slight breeze kicked up the dust around my feet, swirled it into a miniature dust devil, and pushed it toward the river's dark water.

I could hear the voice of the wind. My skin prickled and the hair on my arms and the back of my neck rose. I recalled Old Simon telling me the indios could hear the voices of the earth, the soil, the rocks, the trees, the river.

And the wind.

The breeze grew in intensity, rattling the álamo's leaves above my head. The wind sang these words: *Vaya cuando puedes, vaya cuando puedes.* Go while you can, go while you can.

Then, suddenly, it stopped. The dust settled at my feet, the leaves ceased their motion, and quiet surrounded me, embraced me, as though all sound had drained from the world. I stood, shivering. I looked down at Pete and saw him shudder as though visited by spirits.

When I turned to leave, the goatherd had circled back. He was close enough for me to see the white teeth of his smile and a silvery, stitched, crucifix-shaped scar on the right side of his face. He stood motionless and regarded me for a long while. Then he nodded and I nodded back.

As I walked away it occurred to me the face of the goatherd reminded me of one I had seen in a recurring dream, one that had visited me for years.

The Discipline

La Disciplina

In the sixth grade at the small, poor Catholic elementary school I attended, I was the second smallest student in the class; only Pee Wee Paris was smaller. Because I was skinny, frail, and kept to myself, the bigger boys picked on me and called me names. Sometimes they caught me on the playground or in the bathroom and beat me.

Weeks of being picked on, of being slapped around, exhausted and frustrated me. I tired of the older boys, tired of the beatings they dished out, and finally tried to fight back. The first time I struck out to defend myself, Sister Lucia grabbed me from behind, twisted me around, and slapped me hard across the face. I stared into her narrowed eyes and tight mouth as she lectured me about fighting. As she scolded, her voice grew loud and shrill, her eyes wide and crazed. She upbraided me for smoking discarded cigarettes, an offense of which I was not guilty. Her screaming increased in volume as her body shook and jerked with agitation. She beat me with closed fists, then with the edge of a ruler that raised welts on my back, face, and arms. As she thrashed me she screeched that the Lord would punish me for my sins.

"You must be disciplined," she said.

I fought free, ran to the edge of the playground, and hid in the willows alongside a cool, narrow stream. Sister Lucia found the priest and told him that I had refused her discipline, and he came for me. Sweating and cursing, the fat, jowly, black-cassocked

Father Bohland found me among the reeds and bushes, dragged me by the collar across the playground, and pushed me into his tiny, windowless room that served as a rectory. Burly, with oversized and dangling earlobes and a five-day growth of beard, Father Bohland closed the door and locked it. The only light in the room came from a dim and fading bulb socketed in a small yellow lamp on his bedside table.

Father Bohland turned from the door and slapped me hard across the face with his hammy hand, knocking me to the floor. He cursed, slurring, and kicked at my ribs and legs and face as I lay balled up, crying for him to stop. From time to time he would stoop over to strike me with his hand.

"You are a miscreant," he shouted. "You are a left-handed child of Satan. You must be disciplined!"

Reeling with pain from the kicks and blows, speechless with fear, I lay silent and still. After catching his breath, the priest picked me up, cradled me in his arms, and placed me atop an aged and worn quilt on his stinking bed. My nose leaked blood that ran into my mouth and onto the dirty, whiskey-smelling quilt.

Breathing deeply, his rage spent, Father Bohland crooned, "God means for this to happen, God wants me to punish you like the others." His eyes narrowing to slits, he said, hissing, "You must be disciplined."

"I wasn't smoking," I said, sniffling. "And I was only trying to defend myself."

As I tried to wipe away tears and blood, the priest placed a heavy hand on my chest and held me down firmly on the mattress.

"Everything will be all right now," he sang. "Just relax. I will be good to you now."

With his free hand, Father Bohland loosened my belt and began probing in my pants.

Frightened, not understanding, I kicked and bucked and fought until I was free. Free from his grasp. Free from his stinking room. Free from the school.

I never went back to this school. At least, not right away.

The Bully

El Matón

One day after school during the autumn I was twelve, I walked along one of the shallow drainage canals between my home and the river. The canal was one of those seemingly endless ditches that carried away excess irrigation water from the vast fields of cotton and alfalfa, water thick with the greenish gray of plant debris and fertilizer.

I was used to spending time alone. I was still small for my age, looking more like I was eight or nine instead of twelve. I liked being alone. I craved the solitude. I found comfort and peace in the quiet world of the canal bank and the company of Pete.

A squeaking sound interrupted my reverie, and I looked up to see Damien Vetter riding his battered green bicycle toward me. Fourteen years old and in the sixth grade, six inches taller than I, wiry, and mean, Vetter held a cigarette between his teeth as he pedaled, his slicked-back, brilliantined black hair reflecting the sunlight.

Though forbidden, Vetter often smoked at school behind the gymnasium and cafeteria, flaunting his bravado and daring anyone to inform the nuns. A bully, he picked fights with others, but always with those like me who were smaller and weaker and reluctant to retaliate. Vetter bragged about the many girls he claimed he bedded, some as old as nineteen. He boasted about the size of his penis, claiming it was bigger than any man's.

My throat grew dry and my heart pumped harder as I watched his approach. During the past two years, Vetter cornered me at every opportunity, slapped me around, and made me give him any change I might be carrying. As he neared, I assumed I was only moments away from another beating. I looked around but there was no one to come to my aid. We were far enough away from the houses that my cries would not be heard. Vetter could kill me and no one would know. I searched the ground near the canal for something to use as a weapon but found nothing. My heart thudded with fear.

Vetter skidded his bike to a halt in front of me, raising dust and scattering gravel. A reptilian smile creased his face, and he narrowed his eyes with exaggerated meanness. Around his neck hung a silver crucifix from a silver chain.

Pete stood near the front wheel of the bicycle yapping a warning. Vetter kicked and spit on him. The little dog backed away but continued barking.

Thrusting his thin, sharp-angled face forward, Vetter said, "Hey, kid! You got any money?"

I reached into my pockets in the hope of finding a few coins that might allay his need and speed him on his way. I found none and held out empty hands.

Vetter reached behind his back and withdrew a knife from his belt, a cheap, rusted hunting knife with a ragged-edged, five-inch blade and broken wooden handle. He waved it in front of my face.

"Do you want to die?" he taunted. "Do you want to die? Do you want me to cut you up into little pieces, you little shit?"

I could not answer. I realized in that instant I was scared not of Vetter, not of the knife, but of his question. I was frightened by my own uncertainty because I did not know the answer.

I realized at that moment that I didn't care whether I died or not, that I had arrived at some threshold where I could no longer endure the hectoring. I knew that if I didn't end it now, I would be victimized by the Damien Vetters of the world for the rest of my life. The decision removed some indescribably heavy burden from my shoulders, and at the same time it occurred to me that fear had kept me from doing things I needed to do, kept me from making decisions I should have been making. I experienced in that instant a sense of freedom that felt delicious, that I never wanted to lose.

I also realized I was goddamned tired of the bullying pissant Damien Vetter.

With the accumulation of months of concentrated anger boiling from within, I reached out and grabbed the bike's handlebars with both hands and shoved hard, pushing the vehicle backward, then sideways, then over, spilling it to the ground. Surprised and off-balance, Vetter tumbled from the bike, his right pant leg tangled in the chain sprocket. As he reached out with his arms to break his fall, he dropped the knife, landed in the dirt, and rolled over onto his back. I snatched the knife from the ground and leaped upon him.

With my knees on his chest and my right hand squeezing his throat, I rammed the point of the blade into his right nostril, thrust deeper, and tore open the entire side of his nose. Vetter emitted a high-pitched, feminine-sounding shriek. I squeezed his throat harder, curling my fingernails into his flesh, cutting off the noise. He tried to speak, but no sound came. His mouth struggled to open and close, looking like that of a landed carp. I tingled with the joy of anticipated revenge.

Blood covered the right side of Vetter's face, his tears mixing into the claret and diluting it. He gasped for air and bucked, trying to throw me off his chest. I pounded his skull thrice with the handle of the weapon and he ceased. Releasing his throat and grabbing a handful of his greasy hair, I placed the sharp edge of the knife against the smooth flesh of his throat. Sensing the steel on his skin, he lay motionless and stared at me, his eyes wide with terror, his body trembling beneath mine. I looked hard into his black eyes and for the first time saw fear in another person, the fear of someone who believed he was about to die. The air grew foul with the stink of his released bowels.

I hated Damien Vetter. I knew that it would be an easy thing, a completely satisfying thing for me, to slit his throat open and watch him bleed to death on the dirt road. I applied a bit more pressure to the rough-edged blade and slid it across his throat just below his Adam's apple, just enough to part the tiny blood vessels, the microscopic nerve endings, but not enough to part the thicker dermis beneath. A thin trickle of blood seeped out and ran onto his upper chest, staining his shirt.

I held the bloody knife up to his face, tiny droplets falling from the blade and striking his cheeks, his eyes. Vetter took a deep breath, shuddered, and passed out. When I felt his body go limp under me, I rose and stood straddling him. I felt no remorse, no pity. Rather, I wrestled with the decision of where to cut him next.

I decided to castrate him.

I cut away Vetter's belt, unbuttoned his Levi's, and, fighting the smell, pulled the denims down to his knees. The blade cleanly sliced away his soiled underpants, which I stuffed into his mouth. Pete dashed up and bit Vetter on the left arm, then the ear.

The size of Vetter's penis was unexpected. It was less than an inch long, a mere rose-colored button resting on the white skin of his hairless groin. Worse, he had no testicles.

"Christ!" I muttered. Denied the pleasure of seeing my revenge out to the end, my breathing slowed and in a few minutes returned to normal.

Stepping away, I threw the bloody knife into the canal. The blood from Vetter's wounds ran from his face and neck onto the ground, seeping into the sand and fingering outward in short, narrow, slow-moving streams until it thickened and stopped.

I kicked dirt at the blood, at Vetter, sprinkling his bloody face with grains of silica that stuck. I untangled his pant leg from the sprocket, lifted his bike from him, and threw it into the canal also. Stepping back to Vetter's side, I jabbed him in the ribs with the toe of my shoe, and he responded with a low moan. I spat on him and Pete bit him again, this time on the face. I turned and walked back up the path, Pete trailing at my heels.

How easy, I thought, how very easy it would be to kill someone.

The Cross

La Cruz

When I was fifteen, I carried Pete's body to the river in a cardboard box, placed him in a shallow hole I dug beneath the álamo grande, and covered him with the warm sand. For a marker, I erected a thin slab of sandstone at the head of the tiny grave. On the surface I scratched his name and the year, 1927. I knelt beside the small mound of earth and cried. Then I said a quiet prayer for the friend who never questioned or condemned, the friend who simply followed me wherever I walked for the sake of companionship, for the sake of adventure.

I sat for hours against the bole of the álamo, staring at the river, at the land beyond. I wondered long and hard at what could be found there in the land that extended southward farther than I could dream.

Clouds formed and the temperature dropped sharply. The wind rose, shaking the limbs of the álamo, lifting and swirling the dust until I could barely see. The wind, loud and insistent in my ears, sang once again: *Vaya cuando puedes, vaya cuando puedes.* Go while you can, go while you can.

Across the river, the pueblo was obscured by dust haze, but rising above the suspended particles, the mission cross shone dull red in the darkness caused by the clouds above and the refracting dust below.

It bled.

The Revenge

La Venganza

For years I had nightmares of the beatings from the nun and the priest, of the holy man's dark, stinking, airless room, the dreams illuminated by the dim, flickering yellow light I remembered emanating from his lamp. As I tossed, restless, in my bed, I heard over and over again the words, *You must be disciplined.*

For years I wanted revenge, wanted to teach the priest that the vile things he did to me, to others, were unacceptable. I planned what I would do. I waited. I grew taller. My bony frame filled out. I toiled in the oil fields, on the loading docks, labored on ranches and farms. I swam long distances in the canals. I worked out at the gym, punching the bags and sparring for hours at a time. I honed my body boxing for money in the rings, the plazas, and the arenas along the border. I tuned my mind fighting in the dangerous Mexican bars and on the mean streets. By fighting, I learned a lot about myself, about what I was capable of. I learned to survive.

One evening just past sundown and seven years after the priest held me down on his filthy bed, I returned to the school. Little had changed, the unpainted stucco walls of the buildings only slightly more weathered than I remembered. I walked across the playground. I went to the place where I had hidden from the nun in the bushes by the creek. I breathed in the familiar smells of water and willows, the wormy, frog scent of the dark, slow-moving water.

I remembered. I remembered it all.

A waxing quarter moon barely illuminated the path to Father Bohland's room. I paused a moment, then knocked on the door. I heard rustling sounds from beyond, and a moment later the door creaked open, familiar smells seeping out from the dingy room—whiskey, sweat, and things unwashed. The same dirty yellow light spilled out of the foul space and onto my shirt.

Drunk, a bit grayer at the temples, red-faced Father Bohland squinted at me, obviously perturbed at being interrupted. He saw not a frail, skinny, sixth grader this time. He saw a denimed, T-shirted, motorcycle-booted, duck-tailed, muscled, determined man with angry eyes.

"What do you want?" he asked, his words slurred with whiskey. A wine stain the size of a hand insulted the black of his cassock.

I smashed the priest's thick, rose-veined nose with my fist. It exploded, spraying blood across his face, his cassock, my white T-shirt. He sprawled backward onto the dirty floor. I stepped inside, closed the door, and locked it. I told him who I was and why I had come.

"There were so many of them," he said, groaning. "How am I supposed to remember you?"

As he struggled to his knees, I kicked him hard in the ribs, feeling the thin bones snap beneath the layer of fat. I kicked at his stomach, face, arms, and legs. I broke more bones. I wasted his blood on the floor, the walls. When I tired of kicking him, I grabbed his jowls and lifted his face close to mine and asked, "Can you hear me?"

He nodded, blood dribbling out of his smashed nose and torn mouth through broken teeth, and onto his chin.

I hissed, "You must be disciplined."

I slammed his head hard to the floor. I rose, stared at his puffed, bleeding face, and felt nothing but rage.

"Please, for God's sake," he rasped through bubbling blood. "Don't hit me any more. Please."

"God? What do you know about God?" I asked. "You throw God out to others as a shield behind which you hide to practice your demented passions on those weaker than you."

"God will protect me," the priest rasped.

"There is no god in this room to protect you from me."

I kicked him hard in the head, rendering him inert. I pulled a Mexican shiv from my boot. The blade, honed for days on Carborundum and leather, gleamed in the light of the bedside lamp.

"May your God have mercy on your rotten soul," I crooned, and pulled back his cassock.

I was about to cut away his undergarments when something stayed my hand. The cutting of Damien Vetter years earlier swirled before me. Unsure, I wavered between revenge and walking away.

Knife in hand, I stared at the semiconscious priest on the floor. Disgusted, I hurled the knife as hard as I could and shattered the lamp, eliminating the shit-yellow glow.

I turned and walked out, walked away into the night.

The Wind

El Viento

For seven years I went to the crossing whenever I could slip away. It was solitude I sought, required, and it was solitude I found at the crossing, hours and hours of sweet, blessed solitude. It became ritual for me; it became solace.

I would sit in the shade of the álamo next to Pete's grave and stare into Mexico across the river. I often stood for an entire afternoon beneath the cottonwood listening intently to the faint strains of voices and melodies that seeped through the trees from the pueblo and drifted across the floodplain. I wanted to know what they were saying. I wanted to know the words to the songs they were singing, to know what they were thinking, what they talked about, what they thought about, how they loved. I listened to the faint, distant strains of music from guitars and accordions. I wanted to know the country beyond the pueblo, far into the desert, into the mountains that stretched hundreds of miles southward deep into Mexico. I longed to go and see for myself.

Each time I came to the crossing the old goatherd was always there. Sometimes he was close, sometimes far away, but each time I saw him, he was watching me, and each time he smiled and waved, I waved back.

When I visited the crossing the wind always found me and sang me the same song: *Vaya cuando puedes*. Go while you can.

The Newspaper Report

El Reportaje

One Friday night a few days after I turned eighteen, I followed my friends—Johnny Red, J. Clovis Meriweather, and Floyd Morganflash—to the international crossing between El Paso and Ciudad Juárez. As was our habit, we parked J. Clovis's car, a black, beat-up 1921 Ford, borrowed from his father, in a vacant lot and walked across the bridge into Mexico. Here we prowled the streets, observing the flow of life and culture, ending up at The Lobby, a club where trumpeter Fernando Archuleta and saxophonist Oscar Marufo, along with a drummer and bass player, played popular dance tunes of the day. The place was thick with dancers and cigarette smoke, the drinks were cheap, and there were opportunities to fight.

Two hours later, having no luck finding sport, the four of us left and walked across the street to La Caverna, a below street-level bar frequented by moneyed El Pasoans. After descending the dark stairway and seating ourselves on plush leather barstools, J. Clovis introduced me to a new experience: my first tequila, a 100 percent blue agave creation that provided me, in turn, with my first drunk. The clear liquid, along with some lime and salt, all yielding a taste of southern Sierra Madre foothills, was a new adventure, one I was unprepared for.

We had been in La Caverna for an hour when I felt a gentle touch on the back of my neck. I turned to see a striking woman standing beside me, her short black hair and black eyes a dramatic contrast to porcelain white skin. Her low-cut blouse and knee-length skirt revealed smooth, blemish-free flesh and suggested pleasures I'd only read about, heard about. She smiled and flirted. Too inebriated to understand much of what she was saying, I was flattered by her attention, warmed by her smile, stirred by her touch.

Two drinks and some pleasant conversation later, a burly, red-haired man stepped between us and with barely contained rage told the woman he had been walking up and down the main street looking for her. He struck her across the face with the back of his hand and demanded she explain why she was here in this dark, smoky bar. Before she could answer, he wheeled around, placed his angry, freckled, scowling face close to mine, and said, "You son of a bitch! What do you think you are doing with my wife?"

Senses dulled by drink, I only smiled and shrugged.

Gesturing with his fists, he dared me to step outside into the street, adding, "I'll teach your skinny ass to mess with my wife."

Finding no reason to waste time and energy by climbing back up the stairs, and irritated by him striking the woman, I straight-armed him in the mouth with the heel of my hand, felt some teeth dislodge, and sent him crashing backward to the floor. Adrenaline surged through my veins, displacing alcohol. Leaping from the barstool, I landed on the husband swinging my fists, connecting with his face and head. The last thing I remembered was being surprised at how much blood flowed from his mouth and nose.

• • •

Late the following morning, I awoke in a strange room, naked under a sheet. Sore and stiff, every muscle ached. Bruises covered my face and body. My throat was dry and scratchy from the margaritas. I tried to rise but found it difficult and painful, so I called out. Moments later, J. Clovis, grinning, walked in with a cup of steaming coffee and the morning newspaper.

"Hell of a fight," he said. "I was certain he was going to whip you good until the two of you rolled into the ladies' restroom and you wedged his head between the commode and the wall and began strangling him. Me and Johnny Red thought you had killed him, so we gathered you up and carried you out before *la policia* arrived. I didn't figure your mother needed to see you looking this way so I brought you here. My mom is fixing us breakfast, some huevos rancheros and fried potatoes."

Hours later, refreshed from a good meal and more sleep, I sat on the Meriweathers' back porch and nursed my throbbing headache and sore muscles. I unfolded the *El Paso Herald Post* and read a front page special report:

March 17, 1930

MEXICAN PEASANTS SLAUGHTERED IN LAND GRAB

Numerous reports of raids on peasant villages in the foothills of the Sierra Madres in the Mexican states of Chihuahua and Sonora have recently filtered across the border into El Paso. The raids are allegedly conducted by mounted and armed employees of wealthy landowners in the region, ranchers who have tried for years to acquire the historic communal homelands of the mestizos.

Dozens, perhaps hundreds, of peasants who opposed the ongoing and brutal attempts at takeover have been dragged from their homes, subjected to torture, and sometimes killed in front of their families.

At stake are tens of thousands of acres of arable land in the possession of the peasants, land that is desired by the ranchers, many of whom maintain strong political ties with the Mexican government.

In response to the raids, small bands of rebel forces have formed to fight the landowners and their private armies, some of which have been supplemented by Mexican soldiers.

One such band of guerilla fighters is led by a man known only as Chávez, believed to be a Yaqui Indian. According to Rafael Gonzalez, an El Pasoan with relatives in Chihuahua, Chávez's parents, brothers, sisters, wife, and three small children were all slaughtered during an attack on the village of San Luis in the foothills of the Sierra Madre Occidental.

Chávez, called the Mexican Robin Hood, is believed to be responsible for the retaliatory slaying of approximately twenty men in the employ of one landowner, Joaquín Mueller.

A reward of $10,000 is being offered for the elusive Chávez, dead or alive.

The Decision

La Decisión

Almost a year out of high school, I'd been working jobs where I could find them: digging postholes and stringing barbed-wire fence on neighboring ranches, hauling hay bales, cleaning out barns, sport fighting in Zaragoza, Las Palomas, and Juárez, and working on the loading docks and oil fields.

I found no satisfying work in the land of opportunity and was going hungry in the land of plenty. I felt chained and shackled in the land of the free and encountered a plentitude of cowards in the home of the brave. I'd even been thrown out of the house of the Lord.

I was growing weary of having my attitudes shaped by platitudes and my patriotism fired by slogans and clichés while the rich got richer, the poor got poorer, the lines got longer, the jails more crowded, and people drove faster, going nowhere, getting nowhere, and dying younger, more violently and more often.

On a cool spring morning, hands shoved deep into denim jacket pockets, I leaned against the álamo's rough bark and stared at the river. Texans thought of the Río Grande as a boundary between two countries and little more, a line across which one was not allowed to cross. Many farmers and ranchers saw it as a source of water with which to irrigate the vast fields lying on both sides of the border.

Conversely, Mexicans perceived the stream as a small obstacle, something to cross to get to the other side, perhaps to a better life.

When I came to the river that day, my impulse was to cross, to see what waited for me in the far reaches to the south. Mexico was pulling me, and Texas was pushing.

The wind ruffled the álamo's leaves overhead, a light wind that carried aerosols of dust past my eyes. Its muffled song, now familiar, came from afar, but increased in volume as it gained velocity. Then, it was upon me again, singing *vaya cuando puedes, vaya cuando puedes.*

I knew I would not be able to resist much longer.

The Goatherd

El Cabrero

I didn't tell my friends. I didn't tell Old Simon. I didn't even tell my mother. I didn't bother with paperwork, a passport, a visa. I just knew I had to go, to cross, that it was time.

Standing beside the álamo, hands in my jacket pockets against the cold, I watched a lone Mexican golden eagle soaring high above the floodplain on the opposite side. Lost in reveries of flight and freedom, I heard only the sounds of the river and the wind.

I felt his presence before I saw him. I looked around to find the old goatherd standing beside me, leaning on his staff. Goats milled about, grazing on the lush floodplain grasses, browsing the brush that grew along the riverbank.

Close up, the weathered countenance of the goatherd was benevolent. Dressed in ragged clothes and wrapped in the moth-eaten serape that hung below his knees, I guessed him to be about seventy-five years old. His piercing Indian eyes glowed like coals and sliced the space between us. I noticed again the crucifix-shaped scar on the side of his face and wondered at its origin.

Holding his gaze steady, the old man looked up at the eagle, watched it a moment, then turned toward me and spoke for the first time.

"If you want to fly with the eagles," he said, "you must learn to live like one. *El águila* is an opportunist and a killer, a raptor of black and gold, a fierce hunter that rips and tears its prey. Yet, it is gentle with its young. *El águila* is silent and strong. It attacks prey many times its size. It does what it can to survive.

"Can you do it?" he asked, cocking a brow. "Can you fly with the eagles?"

"I am consumed with a passion to fly with the eagles," I replied. "It crowds out other dreams at night. It seeps through my pores. Like the sweat of the honest bracero it cannot be held back. Yes, I can do what it takes to survive. I can fly with the eagles. I know this."

"*Pues*," he said, "*buena suerte*." Well, good luck.

I shouldered my pack stuffed with a woolen serape, a change of socks, and some leftover biscuits. I pulled my battered straw hat down low and tight, took a deep breath, and walked toward the crossing.

I wondered if I told the old man the truth.

The River
El Río

Stepping off the bank, I lightly probed with the toe of one booted foot until I found the gravel bar lying unseen only inches below the surface of the brown, turbid water. Stepping onto it, I paused, took a deep breath, then proceeded with short, halting steps toward Mexico. Halfway across, the current, thick with silt and debris, deepened and swirled around my thighs, tugging me downstream. Leaning slightly into the current, I continued on. A sudden gust of wind threatened my balance, but I maintained my footing, sliding my feet carefully across the rocky underwater connection.

The water was warm for March, warmer than the air above it. The gravel bar beneath my boots became smoother as I neared the south bank, the slope of the river bottom rising gradually. I paused for a moment to look downstream, saw the river disappear beyond a bend in the distance. With its innumerable fords, I knew people had crossed this river in both directions for centuries. Where were they going? What were their reasons? Like me, had they heard the call of the wind?

As I made my way toward the south bank of the Río Grande, I felt a sense of anticipation, though of what I knew not. Twice I stopped to look back at the land I had just left. It would be an easy thing to turn around and go back, but I knew I could not.

Like the current that was pulling me in a downstream direction, Mexico likewise pulled me to her bosom southward.

The Other Side

El Otro Lado

On reaching the opposite bank, I turned to wave at the old goatherd, but he was gone. I searched the plain upstream and down as far as I could see, but there was no one, nothing but the grass and the álamo. No goatherd, no goats. It was as if he had never been there.

I dropped my pack and sat down on the sandy bank and unlaced my boots and removed them, pouring out the dirty water. I pulled off my socks and wrung them dry. The morning sun warmed the desert air, so I laid back and allowed it to dry my feet and pull some of the moisture from my Levi's. The growing warmth suggested a nap, but the excitement of the crossing prevented one.

I noticed the change in the air the moment I stepped onto the southern bank after crossing the river. I had lived in the desert for a long time. I had grown accustomed to various scents carried by the wind and recognized many of them. The pungent aroma of creosote bush greeted my nostrils. I smelled spring flowers fresh out of the ground.

But there was more, much more. I had grown to detect the difference between the smell of love and fear, both of which are married to the Mexico air.

The Chihuahuan dryness robbed moisture from the soil, the streams, the trees, the brush, from the people who lived here, moisture carried away by the erratic, swirling currents of air. The air seemed to move with an underlying urgency. Sometimes it moved with violence.

The air carried sand and dust. It carried the smell of animals, alive and dead. Sometimes it carried the smell of men, alive and dead.

Whether advecting across the sandy wastes and plains or dancing through glades, the Mexican air carried the smell of danger. Always danger.

I replaced my socks and boots, hoisted my pack, and started out across the floodplain toward the pueblo beyond the line of álamos. I could see the cross rising above the treetops.

The Arena

La Arena

Wind-whipped dust crowded into the tiny border town that lay beyond the álamos on the Mexican side of the river. Still damp from the crossing, I walked through the shadow cast by the large church and felt a chill shiver slowly down my back. Though less than twenty minutes from Juárez by car, the town of Contreras had no electricity and only hand-dug wells and septic pits. A pair of mule-drawn wooden carts and a lone burro moved along the dirt streets, mute company for the dogs that moved from one patch of shade to another as the mood struck them and the chickens that pecked at insects in the dirt.

The wind carried the sweat-smell of working men and the aroma of cooking meat. Wary of intruders, these border folk eyed me with quiet and not unfriendly suspicion. On the wooden door of a cantina was tacked a bright *noticia* advertising a boxing match between Pablo Ortiz and Ramón Samaniego to be held at the Armendáriz barn. At the bottom of the colorful poster was the name Alberto Mendoza, Promoter. Mendoza booked most of the matches I fought along the border, and I decided to see if I could find him to schedule an additional fight where I would go against a local pugilist and earn a few pesos.

I found an old man taking sun on a hand-carved wooden bench in the small, grassless plaza and asked him if he could tell me where to find Armendáriz's barn. He nodded and pointed toward a plank structure, gray with age, near the eastern edge of the pueblo.

"Is Mendoza in town?" I asked. The old man nodded again and gestured toward the barn.

Mendoza stood in the wide doorway of the building as I approached. A small man less than five-and-a-half-feet tall, he arranged fights in the arenas, plazas, and *palenques* located along the border from Las Palomas to Nuevo Laredo. He smiled at me, curiosity in his eyes as he looked over my pack and drying pants.

"Your presence here is a surprise," he said.

"I need a fight," I told him. "I need money."

"You are in luck," he said. "A fight is scheduled for tonight, but one of the *combatientes*, Samaniego, has not shown. Would you be willing to take his place?"

• • •

Just past sundown I entered the barn with Mendoza. The air was heavy and dank. A mixture of smells permeated the old building, many I could not identify. Half the small town was already seated on the wooden benches and chairs, the men drinking cerveza, homemade sotol, and tequila.

Mendoza rolled and lit a foul-smelling cigarette that smelled vaguely of horse shit and led me to the arena. In the middle of this mill-timbered barn, dimly lit by kerosene lanterns, was the palenque, the circular pit where the cocks fought on weekends. I stared, sniffing once again the diffused scents, the smells of animals, of men, of stale liquor and tobacco, of dark earth mixed with blood.

"Tonight you fight Ortiz, the local champion," Mendoza said. "He is *muy mal hombre*. He works in the fields by day and on weekends carries rock for the village stonemason. He is built like a bear with fists the size of cantaloupes. He seldom loses a fight."

Mendoza paused long enough to take a deep drag on his cigarette, smiled, and said, "Ortiz is a killer."

Aren't they all? I thought.

Secure in the knowledge that their hero, Ortiz, would defeat me handily, perhaps even injure or kill me, the eyes of those who came to watch looked upon me with pity. A few whispered, their hushed conversation punctuated with laughter as they pointed at me. None of them believed I had a chance.

I stripped off my denim shirt, boots, and socks and entered the palenque wearing only my Levi's. Mendoza slipped eight-ounce gloves over my freshly wrapped hands and laced them, checking his knots over and over. The well-used gloves were torn in several places and contained just enough padding to keep me from breaking a knuckle, but not enough to keep from breaking Ortiz's nose or jaw.

With gloves secure, I turned to see Ortiz approaching the pit from the opposite side of the barn. Confident, he strode forward in the murky light. Ortiz was huge, at least four inches taller and forty pounds heavier than me, with broad, bull-like shoulders and massive hands, and layered in muscle. He moved with assurance, but I suspected he carried more weight than his legs were capable of handling with ease in the ring. I was confident he lacked my quickness and agility. I believed I could take him, that I could kill him if I wanted to, but I would have to stay away from those huge fists that looked as if they could smash the head of a steer.

No three-minute rounds. No bell. No referee. These fights followed border rules, the end coming only when one of us could no longer rise.

A man in a ragged, faded blue suit of cheap cloth beckoned Ortiz and me to the center of the pit where we halted three feet apart. We eyed one another. We evaluated. I sensed power in his rippling, field-hardened, sloping shoulders and his long, heavy arms. Ortiz smiled at me. A smile of contempt.

The man in the suit barked a command and we fought. The shouts of the crowd rose, then faded somewhere into the back of my mind as Ortiz and I circled, I dancing on the balls of my feet, he shuffling elephantlike in the dirt of the pit. Like distant muffled drums, pulsing like the beat of a heart, the roar of the spectators sounded as if it traveled through water. I danced to the beat.

Ortiz was quicker than I thought possible. We circled for long minutes, jabbing and feinting. Once, when he blocked a hard blow with his shoulder, it felt like striking the trunk of an oak. I knew I had to go after the softer, more vulnerable places.

His punches lacked accuracy and slid off me as I read his movements, twisted with them, causing him to strike empty air. Yet, when he connected, it was with a force that knocked me backward several steps. No rhythm, no timing, but great power. *I must be careful of his power.*

Ortiz charged, I evaded. I struck, he countered. After eight minutes we breathed heavily, trying hard to replace lost oxygen. He showed no signs of slowing or weakening. I chopped at his face with a succession of lightning jabs and crosses, bringing blood from his lips, nose, and brows.

An unanticipated punch hammered me square in the chest and knocked me to the ground. Breathless, dazed, I rose to my knees in a swirl of dust and cock feathers stirred by the fall. I took my time getting to my feet, sucking air into my lungs.

Ortiz smiled again, spat blood into the dirt at his feet, and allowed me to stand. That was his first mistake.

Doubled over, feigning pain, I lured him closer and smashed my left fist into his throat with an iron-rod blow that came from clear off the ground, all my weight and hostility behind it. Startled, eyes glazing, Ortiz took one step toward me, his legs rubbery, his arms hanging limp at his sides.

That was his second mistake. With a calculated sinistral cross, I crushed his nose, flattening it across his face, shoving fine splinters of bone into his head. Gouts of blood splattered his face and chest, splashed my chest and Levi's. His legs wobbled as I drew back. I sensed something was wrong, but before I could deliver another blow, his knees buckled and he collapsed into the feathers and dust that swam in the pit.

Ortiz's second rushed into the palenque and stood between me and the fallen fighter. The man in the cheap blue suit waved me back and I walked over to stand by Mendoza. The shouts of the onlookers, the bettors, intensified with anger.

Ortiz lay motionless in the center of the pit, blood pouring from his nose. Other men entered the pit and kneeled over the fallen fighter, trying to revive him. A moment later, his second and two others dragged the limp form away. A spotty, medial trail of blood ran between the furrows cut by his heavy heels. As I watched, Mendoza removed my gloves and cut away the wrappings. After wiping Ortiz's blood from my face and chest with a stiff, dirt-encrusted towel, I pulled on my shirt and boots, placing my straw hat on my head.

While Mendoza collected the bets from the furious campesinos, I studied an old, hunchbacked *viejo* who entered the pit with a rake, its handle splinted and taped in the middle. He smoothed out the tracks in the sand, mixing in the blood and feathers. My chest ached. I could scarcely breathe. Mendoza returned and counted out my share of the money—eighteen dollars worth of pesos.

From the rear of the barn where they had taken Ortiz, the quiet murmurings of concern were shattered when the screams and cries of a woman erupted through the dimness. I stared hard into the dark, milling shadows where a huddle of men surrounded the unmoving, prostrate fighter. I glanced at the few glaring faces of the people who remained in the seats. I pocketed my pesos and picked up my pack to leave.

Mendoza placed a hand on my shoulder and said, "Another fight, another victory, amigo. But the most difficult part is about to begin."

My eyes applied for an explanation. Leaning closer, Mendoza whispered, "Ortiz is dead. You have just killed their champion, their brother, a husband and father. You have robbed them of the only thing of which they had to boast. And now, *compadre,* you must walk back to the border... alone."

The Road
El Camino

The narrow dirt road I chose to walk out of Contreras on did not lead back to the border. Instead, it snaked in the opposite direction, crossing a few improved roads as it meandered miles to the southwest and into the Sierra Madres, linking the tiny pueblos found along the eastern slopes of the mountain range. The lonely road, a seldom used artery, wound far to the west of the paved highway that accommodated travelers hurrying between El Paso and Ciudad Chihuahua.

Walking out of the pueblo, I stopped often, turning to stare back in the direction of the river. Back there was the only home I'd ever known. It was still close and tempting, safe. In the opposite direction was the unknown, vague and daunting.

It was dark by the time I reached the edge of Contreras, and I decided to stop at the campo santo to spend the night. I knew la gente would not look for me there. I was tired, bruised, and sore, and needed rest. Huddled behind a headstone, listening to the cemetery wind, I watched thin clouds crossing the quarter moon before falling into an unsettled sleep. I dreamed of Ortiz, his bloodied face, his body, unmoving, lying on the dirt floor of the palenque.

Waking just as the sun cracked above the eastern horizon, I looked around at graves adorned with handmade headstones and statues of Jesus, Mary, and the saints. The campo santo was a sculpture garden. Many plots were dressed with bouquets of flowers, most long dead and dried. Few of the *lápidas* carried an epitaph, only the name of the deceased and occasionally the dates of birth and death. Here was Olguín, there an entire family named Soto, beyond was Macias. Directly in front of me was another family plot, all named Ortiz.

The dead were buried within a few dozen yards of where they were born and where they lived their entire lives, their grave markers constructed and erected to win the favor of those who ruled the afterlife. Later this day, most likely, Ortiz's family would bring him here wrapped in a blanket and lower him into a hole in the ground next to his kin.

After hoisting my pack and preparing to depart, I spotted a youth riding a gray burro along the trail from the south. I approached and asked if he knew the wife of Pablo Ortiz.

"*Sí*," he replied. "She is my *tía*." My aunt.

I counted out ten dollars worth of the pesos given to me by Mendoza, tied them into my bandanna, and asked him to deliver them to the woman. He smiled and nodded, said he would, and urged his burro down the trail toward the village.

• • •

In the sloping, rocky foothills of the Sierra Madres, the road wound along edges of deep canyons. Below, in the shadowed recesses of the fluvially carved and sculpted gorges lay skeletons of horses, mules, and oxen, all victims of misstep. Among these *huesos* were some that looked vaguely human, but I was too far away to know for certain.

Now and again I passed isolated adobe dwellings with small garden patches nearby and a few goats grazing. Often no one could be seen; other times dark faces peered from deep within the shadows of the casas.

The narrow dirt road, now little more than a trail barely suitable for carts, paralleled the strike of the sierras, weaving in and out of the bajadas and piedmonts, and occasionally in the deep shade of canyon and arroyo. Often clear and easy to follow, at other times it was confusing, with other trails weaving and winding, branching and anastomosing, crossing and recrossing. Sometimes the road simply disappeared, and I lost my way only to find it again hours later.

I was not frightened, but I felt troubled by a strange isolation that came from not knowing where I was, where I was going.

The road passed a number of uninhabited pueblos long abandoned because of drought or earthquake or raid, their campo santos left untended, weeds growing up between the neglected, tilted headstones.

I had no notion of a destination, only that the road led in a south-southwestward direction and was taking me deeper into the mountain range. The relatively level plain of the desert had given way to rolling foothills rich with oak, pine, spruce, and many low-growing trees I could not identify. In the distance, the outline of the Sierra Madres' higher peaks kissed a deep cerulean sky. As I walked, herons flew in and out of the wooded bottomlands to the east. Falcons, hawks, eagles, and vultures steered above the undulating flanks of the mountains. In the trees, songbirds I could not name trilled melodies bright and fresh and new to me.

Within the first few days, I exhausted my small store of food and thereafter subsisted on snared rabbits and rock-killed rattlesnakes that I skinned, cleaned, and roasted over an oak fire. Wild onions and grapes grew abundant in the shaded canyons. Spring water, clear and cold, resonated down the slopes of the Sierra Madres.

• • •

Weary from long hours of walking, I awoke one morning from a deep sleep with the warm sun on my face and a large rattlesnake coiled next to me. Thick-bodied, five and a half feet long, and with a head the size of my fist, the Mexican *cascabel* blended harmoniously with the colors of the soil and leaves.

The cascabel was only six inches from my neck, its triangular head resting atop the coil, the forked tongue licking the air. A slight movement from me was responded to with the head rising some five or six inches above the coils, the loud buzzing of the serpent's rattles an acute insult to the warm, soft Mexican dawn.

As I raised my own head, the snake pointed its nose and tongue directly at my face, the slitted, unblinking eyes looking directly into mine. I feared moving any more, afraid to encourage a strike. My heart tapping hard against my ribs, I wondered if this was where I would die, this place so far from my home, my mother.

The rattling continued as the snake tightened its coil, preparing to strike. I was steeling myself to execute a quick roll away from the serpent when it inexplicably slithered out of its convolution, moved leisurely in the early morning coolness, and disappeared into some ground-hugging bushes.

• • •

Days passed when I saw no one. When I did encounter travelers, most were on foot. A polite nod and a simple "*buenos días*" served as a greeting when we passed.

Once, however, a crudely fashioned wagon pulled by two mules came up behind me, and I stepped aside to allow passage. The weathered driver and the wrinkled woman next to him did not look up. As the wagon creaked past, I stared into the bed and saw two dead men, their heads and bodies covered with greasy blankets, their dirty, calloused feet exposed and pointed toward the sun.

• • •

Sundown came early on the eastern slope of the Sierra Madres, and with it came the sharp cold of the evening. At night, seated close to a low fire to ward off the chill, I questioned my journey. But I had no answers. I only knew I had to go.

Wrapped in my serape and huddled under the spreading branches of a large *roble*, oak tree, I heard the cry of a she-fox, the scream of a cougar, the shriek of what I later learned was a jaguar.

Once I thought I heard the wail of a train whistle far to the east. I listened harder, but I did not hear it again and I was glad. It was the loneliest sound I had ever heard.

I thought about the dead men in the wagon. Death, in stark contrast to the thick-boled, sap-rich pines and spruces growing high upon the slopes, was a prominent feature in this landscape.

I lay awake all night remembering my multicolored wallpapered bedroom, my brother and sister laughing, my mother in the kitchen cooking and singing the French songs of her childhood.

The Headstone

El Lápida

Seven steps from the trail a simple marker of old, highly weathered sandstone bore an inscription I could barely read:

Porfirio Lucero
Born Nov. 1910 Died Aug. 1923
Killed By His Father

I stood with my back to the wind, collar up, hat pulled low and tight, chilled hands deep in my pockets, and listened to the silica sound of the sand striking the stone near my feet.

I knew I would not attend my father's funeral when the time came, wouldn't even care that he died since he was little or nothing to me, never had been.

He returned once when I was three years old, stayed for a few weeks, then left for four more years. He never said anything to me, never even said goodbye. He just walked away.

He left my mother nothing—no money to pay the rent, no money for food, no encouragement, no love. I never understood why she loved him, why she ever trusted him, stayed with him, ever cared if he returned or not. I never believed he was worth the effort since he was never concerned for us. I rarely saw him, and on those few occasions when he did come home, he was impatient, angry, always irritated with me and my brother and sister though we tried to stay away from him. I only wanted him to leave.

I never saw my father when he wasn't drinking—beer, whiskey, gin, more beer. My father's drinking made me thirsty, not for liquor but for the sun, the wind, the rain, the desert air, the horizons that stretched in all directions away from him.

I imagined my father's death, a death I often wished for. I imagined a phone call telling me he had died. I imagined hitchhiking down a highway that bisected some little town where he was buried. I imagined asking a gas station attendant for directions to the cemetery and, after searching, finding a marker with his name, date of birth, date of death.

I imagined standing at the foot of my father's grave waiting for some feeling to burst forth, but there was none.

There was only the wind, the desert wind.

With nothing to do, no place to go, I imagined myself turning and walking away.

The People

La Gente

After many weeks, many miles, the road I followed diminished to little more than a seldom-used, weed-shadowed path, one that was often rough and rocky, here and there portions of it completely eroded away by rains and mountain runoff, by landslides.

I passed pueblos where I saw men, women, and children working in communal fields, small, patchy expanses of arable land watered from ephemeral streams. Families of as many as ten living in one-room, tumbledown adobes and *jacales*, homes made of earth, rock, cane, ocotillo, and sometimes scrap. I learned to stop and barter a day or two of work in exchange for food—a handful of *tortillas de maíz*, perhaps some squash and chiles, and if I was lucky, some roasted goat meat or chicken.

The work was easy—gathering firewood, mending fences, milking goats, digging the shallow, narrow irrigation canals they called acequias. Every pueblo boasted populations of chickens, stringy pigs, and bony, scabby dogs, all running unencumbered through the streets. Though thin and gaunt and in some ways resembling the hardworking, desert-hardened people who lived there, they invariably ended up in the stew pot.

La gente delighted in telling me tales of pigs driven mad by hunger and attacking unwary drunks and careless children, devouring them and leaving nothing but clean, white bones. One evening, they said, a village elder was pouring feed into a pig enclosure when he suffered a seizure and fell among them. In the morning his family found only a few pieces of white bone and shreds of his clothing.

Every pueblo, no matter how small, had an *iglesia*, always the largest structure in the village. As la gente passed by the church, they would glance up at the tall crucifix projecting from the apex and cross themselves in the name of the Father, the Son, and the Holy Spirit before passing by. To the church went a percentage of their labor—corn, squash, beans, chiles, peaches, a goat, and the occasional hard-earned peso.

Once, in the heat of a long afternoon, I stopped to seek the interior coolness of a church. Here were religious statues and paintings, the icons of the faith. The saints were frowning, looking dire. Most appeared to be in great pain. In the stations of the cross, the Jesus displayed bruises, blood, a look of great despair.

I stared for long minutes at the icons. An elderly campesino devoting what little spare time he had to working for the church, its gardens, its orchards, and its livestock pens, stopped his sweeping when he neared me.

"*Buenos días,*" he said, and I returned his greeting.

Noting that I was lost in the stations, he glanced at them, shrugged his shoulders, and asked, "Where is the joy? Where is the happiness?" He waved a hand toward the stations and inquired, "Is suffering and pain a requirement for getting into heaven?"

The old man paused a moment, looked around the interior of the church as if to ascertain that no one else was about, then continued. "If one does not suffer, can one understand the human condition? If one has not suffered, can one appreciate relief?"

I stared at him, waiting for more.

"We are happiest when we are very young children and when we are very old," he said. "At these times, we are as close as we can get to God on this earth and the farthest from the demands of others."

He smiled, excused himself, and then returned to his chore.

I sat in the front pew wondering if I remembered how to pray. A black-robed priest watched me from the shadows behind the altar, regarding me as if I were a thief. Feeling unwelcome in the house of the Lord, I picked up my pack and left.

La gente always welcomed me, offered me food and blankets and a place to sleep. La gente embraced me, but not once did a priest ever speak to me.

The Monster
El Monstruo

The trail narrowed, twisting, angled and steep, across the pediment as it climbed toward the inselberg. Where the desert lowlands provided yucca, prickly pear, cholla, as well as mesquite, oaks, and cottonwoods, the higher slopes were blanketed with aromatic pine and spruce that thrived on the cooler air and greater moisture.

In the lowlands, the casas were constructed from adobe, sticks, and wattle, with the cooking fires more often than not outside in front. In the higher altitudes, the homes were commonly fashioned from rock, many with fireplaces.

In the lowlands, the water I sipped from pools had been brown, silty, tasting of salt and sulfur. Here the cold running streams reflected the sky and tasted translucent blue. On the floor of the desert I encountered rattlesnakes, tarantulas, scorpions, and giant centipedes. In the soft dirt of the slopes I crossed the tracks of bear, wolf, cougar, and jaguar.

After leaving the last pueblo, I hiked for six straight days without seeing anyone. The climbing exhausted me, and by sundown the high altitude air brought on a deeper chill and a heavier fatigue than what I was used to. One evening I was tempted to stop and build a fire, but the walking kept me warm and a waxing three-quarter moon lit the trail enough for me to make my way without difficulty.

Two hours after the sun had dropped behind the nearest ridge, I spotted the glow of a campfire several dozen yards off the trail among a dense cluster of conifers. Faint sounds that held a vague suggestion of singing filtered through the night air. Leaving the trail and tracking through the labyrinthine maze of spruce and pine, I crept forward, eager to discern if the camp was friendly or a threat. Within forty feet of the fire, I paused to listen. The sounds could have been singing, but in a language I had never heard before. The odd, primitive melody and gibberishlike vocalizing rendered something as ancient as the very rocks that made up the mountains, a stygian, singsong cadence born of pre-Pleistocene time. The atavistic cast of the song chilled me.

Slowly, I advanced. At the third step, my right boot snapped a twig, the sound slicing sharp and resonant through the cold night. I paused, stiffened, and awaited the response I was certain would come.

The singing ceased, and all was silent.

Just ahead I could see a small, fire-lit clearing. I waited. There was neither sound nor movement. There was nothing. Even the night creatures had gone still.

I ventured one more cautious step forward and saw sudden movement out of the corner of my eye, an amorphous form darting toward me in the dark. The skin on my arms, neck, and scrotum prickled. The sight of it, along with the dead silence of the forest, made my stomach leap and my bowels constrict. My thumping heart caused my *camisa*, my shirt, to vibrate as if caught by an evil gust of wind.

Appearing squarely in front of me, having shot out from behind a large roble, was the face of a monster.

The Dwarf

El Enano

What ungodly parody of a human being was this misshapen, humpbacked, grotesque form standing boldly before me? Though my heart slammed in my chest and I felt my eardrums would burst from the pressure, I maintained my ground. Neither the creature nor I moved. I forced rapid breaths, audible gasps that broke the stillness, trying to regain the oxygen that left me at first fright. I worked to control my shaking.

From eight feet away I could hear the creature breathing, but the air that flowed in and out of his lungs generated a metallic rasping sound like the purring of a big cat.

To flee was not a consideration. Prepared to fight, I took one halting step toward the three-and-a-half-foot-tall shape. It tilted its oversized head slightly, and though I could not see its eyes in the darkness, I sensed it regarding me more with curiosity than hostility. It raised an arm, an arm too long for the abbreviated body of the dwarf.

It was a greeting. I responded in like manner.

The diminutive monster wheezed, "*¡Venga!*" Come!

He turned, waving me forward toward the light of the campfire, and shuffled ahead, a simian-scuttling created by crooked legs and a club foot that made a *ssshhhsshhing* sound as it dragged the ground, cutting a shallow furrow in the loamy earth of the clearing. Tire-tread huaraches slapped loosely on his oversized feet.

In the light of the fire, the gargoyle face was dark and pock-marked. The dwarf's one good eye possessed a disarming, mischievous gleam, one that assured a level of harmlessness. His large-brimmed, battered sombrero, seemingly as wide as he was tall, gave him an almost comical appearance. Covering his dirty cotton pantalones and camisa was an even dirtier serape, its original gray color altered and subdued by miles of travel, sleeping on the ground, and the spilled remnants of countless meals. The oddly bent digits at the end of the bread loaf–shaped feet looked fungal-ridden and wormlike. One foot was missing a toe, the other missing two. Each hand had only four fingers.

Whatever curse had been placed upon this unfortunate misshapen soul or his mother, the small fellow appeared to have made peace with his condition.

Pointing to a smoke-darkened and dented metal pot, he uttered a sibilant invitation to eat. The thick, steaming liquid contained lumps that could have been meat, potatoes, or even rocks.

Smiling, he said, "*Ardilla de piedra.*" Rock squirrel.

Plunging filthy, stubby fingers into the pot, he removed a fistful of the pungent stew and dropped it onto a piece of tree bark he claimed from the ground that served as a plate. After shaking the remaining liquid from his hand and wiping it on the serape, he passed the plate to me and made signs with his hands that he wanted me to taste it.

The meat was tough, stringy, gamy. The liquid, seasoned with chiles and salt, had the texture of sandy paste. Though I hadn't eaten a hot meal in days, I gagged down the first bite and nodded a reluctant appreciation. The second bite was not as bad as the first, and soon I was asking for another helping.

While I ate, the dwarf stared, smiling, drooling, looking pleased.

Setting down the bark plate, I said, "*Gracias,*" and motioning that I needed to be on my way, began to rise.

"Nonsense," the dwarf wheezed. "You cannot walk the forest at night. There are bear and jaguar and wolves and worse. You must remain with me and depart at dawn."

He walked over to where I sat and, sounding like a sack of corn dropped from a great height, plopped down onto the ground next to me. His body and clothes emitted an odor of something long dead. When he spoke, fetid breath oozed through rotted teeth, inviting a nausea that I avoided only by turning my head.

Gesturing, he said, "I am called El Enano. My father was a great warrior among the Quechua, my mother a *bruja*, a witch. Before I was born, my father was killed in a battle with a rival tribe. My mother died when I was but a child. Though she was a young woman, it was said she had turned gray and wrinkled and feeble. Her relatives said I caused her death, that I was cursed. They whipped me, stoned me, set the dogs upon me. I fled into the forest."

He paused, looked at the ground, and sighed, then said, "I have few visitors."

I had no response. I wondered what it would be like to live with this kind of pain, the years of rejection. Finally, I thought to ask, "How do you live?"

"I trap the *ardillas* and harvest wild onions and garlic and berries. Chávez brings me beef and pork and tortillas and corn."

"Chávez?" I asked, recalling the name from somewhere.

"*Sí*, Chávez is my friend. A friend to *los defortunados*. When Chávez took me in, there were no more taunts, no more insults. Chávez watches over me. Chávez rides and fights for me. Sometimes, I ride and fight with Chávez. He claims I bring good fortune to his men, to his raids. Dwarves are believed to bring good luck, and tribal elders often pay huge sums to keep one of us in their households. It seems strange, for my life has not always been one blessed with luck."

"Why does Chávez fight?" I asked.

"His family was killed by hacendado Mueller's vaqueros. They used his wife, then skinned her alive. She was hung by the wrists from the limb of a roble that grew in front of their casa. She lived for two days before Chávez returned home from a hunt and found her. She begged him to kill her, but he cut her down and sang to her until she died in his arms.

"Chávez found the severed heads of his three children impaled on fence posts at the edge of his cornfield. He discovered his parents tied to a tree, burned alive by a slow fire. It was said their screams were heard miles away, carried by the night air of the desert. His sister was raped also. When they finished with her, they slit her throat and let her bleed to death on the front step of her home. His brother was tied to a rail fence and lashed with bull-whips. When they tired of whipping him, they used him for target practice. He had over one hundred bullet wounds on his body."

Stunned, I asked, "Why?"

El Enano tilted his large head, eyeing me in my ignorance. He said, "When hacendado Mueller wants something, he simply takes it. He sends his vaqueros . . ."

"Where is Chávez now?" I asked.

"Chávez is everywhere," replied El Enano.

The dwarf reached into a heavy canvas pack, retrieved a crude, handmade fiddle of unfinished wood, and began playing. The sweet melody brought calm to the forest, to the night. Though I intended to remain awake and alert, I pulled my poncho tight against the night chill and nodded on the edge of sleep, caressed by the lullaby.

The Rider

El Jinete

I bolted awake, snatched from a deep sleep by screeching pine jays. Bright sunlight streamed through the tree canopy and into the clearing. I sat up, looked around, and saw no one.

I recalled the previous evening: El Enano, his stories, his stew, his music. Throwing off my poncho and rising, I stretched, dusted off my pants, and called out.

No answer. The campfire was cold. The canvas pack, the fiddle, the dwarf, gone.

I shouldered my pack, made my way through the maze of trees, and found the trail again. For several days I followed a rocky path that wove up and down, in and out of valleys, across rubble-strewn ridges. I slaked my thirst at thin streams and muttered short prayers of thanks at finding them.

Though the slopes of the Sierra Madres were somewhat cooler than the desert below, rattlesnakes abounded. The thick-bodied cascabeles reached lengths of seven feet or more. I often encountered them in clusters and left the trail to pass safely. Often I killed, roasted, and ate portions of the serpents for supper.

One afternoon, weary from walking and with nothing to eat, I reclined beneath a large tree two dozen yards off the trail and fell asleep. An odd, unidentifiable foreboding stirred me back to consciousness. Barely opening my eyes, I saw a man on horseback stopped on the trail just opposite from where I lay in the shade. The horse remained as still as a statue. The rider neither moved nor spoke, only stared. In case he proved to be a threat, I rose and stared back.

His raven-black *castrato* gleamed in the sunlight, its carefully groomed mane and tail feathered downward and danced in subtle rhythm to the light breeze. The hide of the horse rippled with thick, trail-hardened muscle.

The rider's slitted, obsidian eyes held my gaze. The eyes were unforgiving. His mouth cut a thin line below a charcoal moustache. Like the eyes, the mouth was hard.

Black hair spilled from under his sombrero to the middle of his back. On the right side of his face, extending from temple to chin, was a narrow corrugated scar. From eye to ear ran a horizontal counterpart that created a ragged, crucifixlike pattern. Corded muscle and thick veins flowed under the deep brown skin of arms exposed to the sun from a sleeveless, white, peasant camisa. *Bandoleras* gravid with bullets crisscrossed his chest and twin revolvers sat in leather holsters attached to a wide belt. The handle of a large fighting knife could be seen protruding from a belted sheath at his back. A rifle was scabbarded on the right side of the saddle.

The rider stared up the trail, raised his eyebrows slightly, and looked back at me. I responded with a barely perceptible nod to his unspoken question. He patted the rump of his *caballo*, then extended a hand. Lifting me as though I were no heavier than a child, he swung me up behind him and commanded the horse forward with spurred heels. He reached into a pouch and withdrew two tortillas de maíz and some dried goat meat, which he passed back to me.

We traveled wordless for miles. Arriving at the outskirts of a small pueblo, the rider reined up and, with a single look, invited me to dismount. I slid off, regarded the village for a moment, then looked back up at him and said, "*Gracias*."

He offered a nod, then turned his caballo west and rode into the wooded slopes.

The Village

El Pueblo

The people of San Lorenzo invited me to stay and rest for as long as I wished. I inquired about the possibility of a fight in hopes of earning a few pesos. Politely, they told me that the young men who wished to fight traveled many miles to the east to the town of Guerrero to try their luck. I then offered to work with them in their fields in exchange for food and shelter. They agreed and led me to a small, vacant adobe where I dropped my pack. Inside, a pallet and a crudely made wooden chair seemed like luxuries after living on the trail and sleeping on the hard ground for so many weeks.

San Lorenzo boasted twenty-five adobe and rock casas and no more than seventy-five residents. Most of the homes were well constructed and well cared for. Some were stuccoed with a sand and lime mixture and painted white, and a few gleamed bright in the sunlight from recent coats of paint. Fences made from ocotillo, juniper, or cane accented the casas like fine frames complement paintings. Here and there a broken chair or bench rested beside a house waiting for a time when they could be repaired. The ubiquitous dogs alternately slept and searched for new shade or scraps to eat. Chickens appeared to have free access to roads, yards, and even homes. Pigs snoozed in the cool shade of tree or casa.

A willow-shaded plaza afforded a setting for visiting, mostly by a few old men. At the edge of the plaza loomed the church, its afternoon shadow stretching across streets and covering the homes like a heavy woolen blanket.

I walked past the church, spotting a knot of cascabeles warming themselves in the sun adjacent to the west wall. Not far away a shoat rooted along a fencerow. Barking dogs greeted me. Like the chickens, goats enjoyed the freedom to browse wherever they pleased.

I smelled cooking meat and stopped to watch the women warming tortillas on flat, heated rocks and cooking *cabrito* over open fires. Others were tending small vegetable gardens scattered throughout the pueblo and along a nearby creek. Children too young to work in the fields played nearby.

Behind the church stretched a well-maintained orchard containing dozens of peach trees surrounded by a four-foot-high rock wall. I leaned against it to watch the red and gold sunset.

"*Buenas tardes,*" a voice greeted. I turned to see an elderly campesino approaching from the direction of the church using a cane to aid him up the cobbled path.

I returned his greeting and, pointing to the orchard, said, "It's beautiful. Tell me about it."

Pausing, he rubbed a weathered hand across his whiskered jaw and said, "Years ago we tilled the rough earth, mixed in rich manure from our own livestock along with river silt, planted the young trees coaxed to life from seeds imported from Spain and Germany, and watered and pruned and cared for them by hand. Over time we saw large, healthy trees bearing fruit.

"When the fruit is ready, we pick it and pack it into crates that are shipped all the way to Ciudad Chihuahua by wagon, where it is sold to dealers from *los Estados Unidos*. The money goes directly to the church. We, who do the planting and harvesting, the packing and shipping, receive none of it."

Pointing with his cane toward the orchard, he added, "We are even forbidden to eat the fruit that grows as a result of our toil. The priest tells us it is intended for the Lord, though he eats some of it himself."

He took a breath, scratched his cheek, and said, "Once, two boys climbed the wall and picked some peaches. They were caught by the priest who ordered the right hand of each be severed at the wrist to serve as an example to the rest of us. One boy died from the punishment."

The old man looked at the fruit trees, then back at me, and said, "Please, señor, do not enter the orchard."

I nodded. He turned and walked away.

• • •

The next morning I walked to the fields with the men and was handed an oft-splinted hoe. I chopped weeds between the rows of corn, chiles, and *calabazas*. I laughed and sweated with the campesinos, grateful for the opportunity to work, grateful for their friendship.

It was a breezeless afternoon, and shortly after a lunch of roasted chicken wrapped in tortillas de maíz, a pair of young men with cheap black suits, white shirts, and narrow black ties arrived from the north on foot. Spotting us working in the rows, they increased their pace and made their way toward us.

On seeing the visitors, the campesinos whispered, "*Pendejos* Mormons," and made disparaging gestures toward the oncoming missionaries. One told me they walked this road all the way from their *colonias* far to the northeast, visiting the pueblos trying to get la gente to worship in their strange manner.

Fearing a reprimand from the priest for talking to the Mormons, the workers glanced at the church and then scurried away to their adobes.

Left standing alone, sweating shirtless in the sun, I leaned on the hoe and awaited the approach of the two gringos no older than me and just as gaunt and hungry looking. When they were still twenty yards away, they began preaching about the lost tribes of Israel and the evils of the papacy. They spat out the word Catholic as if it were a disease.

I listened politely to the sallow-faced youths for a few minutes, then hied them away, explaining that I was occupied with the more important work of hoeing squash. When they warned me of a fiery end in hell, I just nodded and went back to chopping weeds. As they walked on, I noticed their worn-out shoes parting at the stitching and wondered if the footwear would hold together long enough for the zealots to return to their homes. I looked at my own boots and saw that they were not much better.

• • •

On the fourth morning of my stay at San Lorenzo, as I was preparing to leave, the old man from the peach orchard came to say goodbye. I asked him about the trail I wished to travel.

"*¡Cuidado!*" he warned. "Armed vaqueros from nearby ranchos are tormenting *la gente*." He pointed to two fresh graves in a campo santo on the stony hillside, victims of a recent attack from raiding vaqueros.

I studied the campo santo without speaking. The graves on the hillside outnumbered the population of the pueblo. Many of the graves were small.

"The little graves?" I asked.

"Half of the children die before the age of five," he replied.

"Are there no doctors?" I asked.

"Only our *curanderas*," replied the old man, "but the church forbids the healers to treat the young ones."

Smiling and placing his hand on my shoulder, he handed me a small fiber sack containing tortillas, fresh corn, and cabrito, packed by his daughter.

"*Gracias*," I told him. "It has been good."

"*Vaya con Dios*," he said.

The Rain

La Lluvia

Once again, the trail I walked paralleled the strike of the foothills. During the day it was warm enough to walk shirtless and enjoy the heat of the sun on my skin. Now and then I passed through welcome pockets of coolness in the narrow canyons. No trucks or automobiles crossed this route, only men afoot or on horseback and the crudely made wooden wagons and carts pulled by mules or oxen. Here, la gente lived as they did one hundred years ago and more.

I encountered no other travelers for a week. Then I saw a man coming from a long way off, and I waited by the trail for him. He was very old, the lines on his face reminding me of the cracks and fractures in the granite and limestone of the mountains. He was barefooted, the soles of his feet leatherlike, impervious to the cold and the sharp rocks on the trail. The torn and ragged serape wrapped around him dragged along the ground. He carried a worn and holey canvas bag that hung from a strap across his shoulder.

The old man raised an arm in greeting and I waved back. He paused, eyes curious, but he asked no questions. He looked back down the trail the way he had come and said, "*Es una senda peligrosa.*" It is a dangerous path. Then he walked on.

That night I made camp at a place long used by travelers. I found a stone fire ring with old ashes. The site had been occupied only a week earlier.

With so much sign of bear, jaguar, cougar, ocelot, and wolves, I built a fire to keep the potential intruders away. As I sat close to the blaze to ward off the night chill, I could hear the movements and sounds of the wild ones in the woods, occasionally the howl of a wolf in the far distance. I sensed the dark energy of the mountain. Having eaten all of the provisions gifted by the people in San Lorenzo, I dined this night on another meal of a small rattlesnake and three small wild onions. I was growing tired of the fare.

I awoke at dawn and made the decision to remain and rest for the day in the remote setting. I contented myself with watching the pine jays, swallowtails, and mockingbirds flit through the trees and search for food on the ground. I found pieces of chipped obsidian where some ancient camper once fashioned arrowheads countless generations earlier. I napped twice, each time my sleep filled with hazy dreams of home, my mother, and, once, the goatherd. In the dream, the face of the cabrero faded only to be replaced by the silent rider who carried me horseback to the village of San Lorenzo. In the dream the rider beckoned me, but I could not determine where.

At dusk, I rebuilt the fire. I had no food to cook, but the sound of the blaze, the sight of the burning wood comforted me. The moon rode low on the western crest of the Sierra Madres as a light patter of rain began to fall on the soft, greening grass. I moved from the fire and leaned back into the partial shelter of the bole of a large roble. Snuggled down into my serape for warmth and imagined security, I listened to the lonely sound of the rain as my stomach rumbled.

I thought about my mother, how she provided well for us under the circumstances, how she made small meals appear as feasts. The joy she brought to the table kept us ignorant of our penniless condition. We never knew we were poor because my mother was happy in her own way, and happiness is one of the best distractions from hunger.

• • •

The next day, wet and chilled, I walked into a small village just as the rains came again, this time falling harder. I took shelter in the church, leaned back into a pew, and fell asleep.

The feeling that I was not alone, that I was being watched, woke me. As my eyes adjusted to the darkness of the holy interior, I spotted a rattlesnake coiled on the stone floor in the shadows near the altar, the forked tongue darting out, its sensors tasting the air, sorting out the different textures, my new and strange heat. Outside, the rain beat down. Inside, the silence was primal.

I looked away from the serpent for a moment, and when I glanced back it was gone. The dark form of a priest, his black cassock almost indistinguishable from the shadows, appeared in the same spot. In the dim light that penetrated the building, he took one step forward and gestured that I must leave.

At the door I looked back and saw that he was on his knees before the altar, his head bowed in prayer. I stepped outside, hungry and shivering, and walked on through the rain.

The Jail

La Cárcel

Two days later, the trail crossed a wide, oft-used dirt road, one that led to the town of Madera many miles to the east. From far away I thought I heard the drone of a vehicle on the road. I stopped, staring hard into the distance, and finally discerned a coil of dust stirred up by an old black pickup truck and a half dozen men on horseback. Nearing the intersection, they spotted me standing alone on the trail and sped forward, the riders surrounding me with drawn pistols. They wore the drab gray uniforms of soldiers or police; I could not tell which.

The riders all talked at the same time, each of them issuing rapid-fire commands that I could not understand. One of them brushed past me with his horse, knocking me back. Another slammed the barrel of his pistol across the top of my head, dropping me to my knees. I placed my hand to the wound, and it came away bloody. I rose, staggered a few steps, and another rider kicked me to the ground. When I tried again to stand, two men from the truck piled onto me, hitting me with fists and nightsticks, and tied my wrists behind my back with baling wire. They threw me hard into the back of the truck, slamming my head on the wooden planks. After tossing my pack next to me, the driver turned the vehicle around and drove back toward Madera, accompanied by the horsemen.

• • •

The tiny adobe jail cell was rank with the piss and shit and vomit of previous occupants. Flies besieged me and I grew weary of fending them off. Rats and roaches passed in and out of small openings in the earthen walls where they met the dirt floor. A stoop-shouldered skeleton of a man wearing stained and greasy jailhouse garb shuffled by once a day to pass me a tin plate of watery, sour-tasting frijoles and a moldy tortilla.

"Why am I here?" I asked him.

"¿Quién sabe?" he replied.

For three days I languished in the fetid cell, assaulted by the stench and insulted by the fare. On the fourth day, a trio of men dressed in fresh-pressed khaki pants and shirts adorned with epaulets, medals, and gold braid approached my cell. Each man carried a revolver holstered on his right hip. Halting just beyond the door, they jabbered rapidly among themselves, and I could not find the thread of what they were saying. They gestured and pointed at me, then all laughed as if at some big joke. One of them withdrew a metal key from his pocket and opened the heavy, barred door. Stepping aside, he motioned for me to exit. I picked up my pack and warily followed him out of the *cárcel.*

He led me to a windowless office, seated me in front of a scarred, wooden library desk, and left. Moments later, a fat, tired, sad-eyed man entered, seated himself behind the desk, and shuffled the stacks of papers spread out before him. In broken English, he explained that the police believed I was the *mal hombre* responsible for a train depot robbery during which two employees were shot and killed. The actual robber and murderer had been captured and confessed two days earlier. I was now free to go.

I stared at him. I wanted to ask what had become of the small amount of money they had taken from me when I was arrested, but decided it would serve no purpose. Without a word, I slipped an arm through a pack strap and walked out.

The Indian

El Indio

I was out of jail, but also out of money, apparently out of luck, and close to running out of hope. I stood in the brightness of the warm sunlight on the concrete steps of the cárcel, a delightful contrast to the grimy, pestilent cell. I breathed in lungsfull of delicious fresh air. I wondered what to do, where to go.

Across the street, standing under the overhang of a cantina awning, an Indian stared at me. Even from that distance I could see a silver knife scar on the right side of his face, a wicked cicatrix that extended from his hairline across his cheek and down to the top of his throat. A second scar running horizontal from ear to eye completed the image of a crucifix. Stoic, unblinking, he regarded me with magic intensity, his black eyes burning across the space between us, knifing into mine. Barefooted, he wore a multicolored poncho that hung to his knees and an orange and black band tied around his head. His hair hung to his shoulders.

The Indian crossed the street coming toward me, his eyes never leaving mine, never blinking. With no preliminaries, he stood before me and asked, "Will you ride with Chávez?"

Stunned, unsure of what he meant, I said, "No." Then, realizing what I really wanted, I said, "I just want to go back to San Lorenzo. I want to work in the fields with *la gente*."

The Indian took a deep breath, then said, "San Lorenzo is no more. It was burned, destroyed. Seven men and boys killed, the youngest four years old. Their bodies, stacked on the steps of the church, were set afire. Six women were raped, two of them killed. Another killed herself in shame."

I stood rigid and unmoving and looked at the Indian. Sadness, revulsion, and anger welled up inside me, threatening to spill out into tears. I set my jaw tight in an attempt to maintain composure, to keep my emotions from pouring out into the day.

"Chávez," he continued, "is Indian, like me. He fights for the peasants, the campesinos, against the landowners, the hacendados. We love our land and try to protect it, to hold it. Because of that, our daughters are raped. We are tied to fence posts and lashed for small infractions. Sometimes we are beaten to death. Girls are taken from our homes and made to work as maids in the mansions of the hacendados. They are used by the masters, then passed around to the vaqueros. When they resist, they are killed, their bodies thrown into the river. Wagonloads of grain produced by our sweat and toil are purchased by the hacendados for mere pesos, and sometimes they are taken at gunpoint."

The Indian paused and glared at me, anticipating a response, but I was unable to speak.

He took an angry breath and continued. "But now, Chávez rides! Rapists are dragged from their homes in the middle of the night and castrated. Those who would whip defenseless field hands are hunted, captured, tied, and lashed until their flayed skin hangs in bloody strips from their backs and legs. They are left to bleed, left for the ravens and vultures. Money is taken from hacendados and divided among *los peones* to pay for food and medicine. Churches in league with the hacendados are sacked and the gold crosses, chalices, and idols are melted down, formed into ingots, and given to the poor. *Sí*, Chávez rides. And now, Chávez wishes for you to ride with him."

Sweating in the street, I shifted my feet. "I do not know Chávez," I said. "And Chávez does not know me."

"You know Chávez," he said. "And Chávez knows you."

He smiled, a grudging, thin, silent smile that quickly faded. Then he said, "The days are long, hard, and dangerous. We often go without sleep, without food. Dust and sand cover our clothes, our saddles, our mounts, invade our eyes and throats, find their way into our food, our water. Dust and sand even find their way into our souls. Soldiers, police, and paid trackers are sent by the hacendados to pursue us, to find us, to kill us."

"Chávez is at war with the devil. Chávez sent me. Chávez asks that you ride with him."

I thought of San Lorenzo, my guts twisting. I shook my head hoping to expel the images from my mind, but they refused to leave.

I looked up at the Indian. His black eyes clamped onto mine and would not let go.

I nodded.

The Indian placed his right hand on my chest over my heart and left it there for a moment. Then, he turned and walked down the street, his feet stirring the thick dust.

I followed a few paces behind.

The Camp
El Campo

Pausing only long enough to sleep for a few hours at a time or eat some dried meat he carried, the Indian and I walked westward across thorny plains and desert sands for three days. On the morning of the fourth day, when I thought I could walk no more, we entered a close-walled, shaded canyon through which trickled a narrow stream, its banks thick with watercress and fern. Approaching an oddly quiet camp, I spotted a raven-black caballo tied to a low juniper and realized then that the rider I met days earlier, the silent one who carried me to San Lorenzo, was the man called Chávez.

Men moved about the camp tending horses, braiding ropes, cleaning weapons, fetching firewood, oiling saddles and belts. All of them were hard-faced Mexican Indians, some *puro*, some mestizo. No one spoke, and their appraising eyes, dark as night, focused on me, manifesting cautious curiosity. The aroma of horse and man-sweat and leather assailed my nostrils, as did the scent of cooking meat.

I spotted El Enano seated on a rock by a large cook pot that swung from a horizontal limb wedged into two forked uprights. Seeing me, he broke into a crooked, missing-toothed smile and called out some undecipherable greeting. Blinking wildly with his good eye, he waved me over and pointed to the contents of the pot.

"*Perrito*," he said, stirring the mixture.

Lumps of young dog meat appeared briefly in the stew before settling again to the bottom. Though ravenous, my stomach churned at the thought of dining on canine.

Though the dwarf's face had the look of one who had seen many years, his eye was that of a child—dancing, bright, mischievous. Short, sparse, bristly hairs grew out of his chin, but it was impossible to discern his age.

El Enano grasped my arm and said, "It is good to see you, amigo. I am glad you are here, with us." Then, he returned to his cooking.

The Indian handed me a canteen of water. As I drank, he nodded toward El Enano and said, "The little man has power, a magic most of us don't understand. Once, I walked into a canyon not far from here and found him there talking to the birds and the birds talking back to him. I watched in silence for a long time.

"He is a *curandero*, a physician. A few weeks ago, Mata and Manriquez returned to camp with serious wounds. Mata's foot was shattered by a vaquero's bullet. We dulled him with mescal and held him down while Herrera lopped off his foot at the ankle with a machete and El Enano cauterized the amputation with the flat side of another machete heated on the fire. Mata died a week later, but Manriquez lived. El Enano cured the blood poisoning in his wounded leg and sent him back to his home in Delicias. The little man knows how to heal. At night he plays the fiddle. He relaxes our bodies. He cures our souls."

I looked away for a moment, watching the men moving about the camp. When I looked back, the Indian was gone.

• • •

Around noon, Chávez appeared, walking into the camp from the direction of the canyon. I had not seen him since I arrived, but suddenly he was there, standing a few yards away, looking tall for an Indian, bent-legged, monkey strong.

Chávez nodded at me, an invitation to follow him as he walked toward the remuda. There, a dozen mountain-bred horses—thick-chested, heavy-rumped, short-legged, and wiry-haired—were strung to a picket line, a tall, rangy Indian tending to them.

Pointing to the man, Chávez said, "This is Olguín."

Olguín looked up at me, glared, then returned to grooming one of the animals. A thickly muscled man who walked with a bowlegged gait, Olguín's right eye was half-closed from thick scar tissue as a result of an old wound just below the brow and in the socket. He had the darkest skin of all of the riders and was missing several teeth. Those that remained were black. Olguín gave off an odor of one who seldom, if ever, bathed. I soon found him to be aloof, distant to all, taking his meals away from the others. Olguín had a cruel manner with the caballos, striking one or another with his fist or a stick, malevolence in his eyes. I learned he was also a vicious fighter and killed with passion.

Stopping in front of a stout brown and white paint, Chávez spoke softly and breathed into the nostrils of the animal as if the two were kin. He stroked the forehead between the eyes and scratched behind its ears. He embraced the horse as if it were his own child.

Turning, Chávez pointed beyond my left shoulder to a saddle with a saucer-sized horn, a bridle, and saddlebags, all straddling a log. Aged, well used, the saddle manifested a scarred rawhide housing held together with some whang. The stirrups were tapadero-rigged and hand-carved from pecan wood.

Though Chávez said nothing, his message was clear—this was my mount, that was to be my saddle.

Calling to Borrego, Chávez bade him come near. Borrego was as tall and as well built as Chávez and walked with a slight limp, yet manifested agility. He had a broad, round face, more Indian than mestizo, that was cratered with poxlike scars. Short, stiff, spikes of unevenly cut hair stuck out from under his dirty felt sombrero, looking more like porcupine quills than locks. On the back of Borrego's right hand was a large, crude tattoo of a spider, the dark head and thorax covering most of the flesh, with five of the legs extending down the tops of his scarred, rough fingers and thumb, the remaining three climbing up the wrist and onto the forearm beneath the sleeve of his camisa. Borrego, I was to learn, was fiercely loyal to Chávez, having lost some of his family members to the vaqueros in a manner similar to the leader. In time, I grew to know him as a silent, competent fighter, a dependable member of the band. I rarely heard him speak to anyone.

Chávez and Borrego spoke in soft tones, the latter glancing at me with suspicion. He left, then returned minutes later carrying a pair of knee-high leather riding boots, campesino pantalones, and a camisa. Chávez gestured that I should change out of my own worn, ragged garments. Wordless, Borrego handed them over.

I donned the used clothes and placed the remnants of my own in my pack. The lace-up boots that had served me well on my journey had large holes in the soles and were coming apart, the stitching unraveled in several places. The heel on one was completely missing.

Though well laved and smelling sun dried, the camisa handed to me had bloodstains on the front. Where the cloth caressed my left nipple, there was a bullet hole. The boots, fitted with heavy spurs and oversized rowels, jingled with every movement.

El Enano stepped forward and handed me a battered felt sombrero, which I placed on my head.

When I appeared in the garb of the riders, Chávez said, "They fit you well. But we do not know yet if you can ride and fight."

Behind him, Borrego grinned. I said nothing, only returned Chávez's stare.

"*¿Cómo se llama?*" Chávez asked. What are you called?

"Carlos," I replied. Though a gringo, I gave him the name I was called in the Mexican neighborhood where I grew up.

"*Bueno*, Carlos, try out your mount."

I spoke to the paint in soft tones, touching him with my hands as I moved about him, saddling and bridling. I placed my head close to his, letting him smell me. I led him around in wide circles several times, allowing him to experience my appearance, my demeanor. I mounted and rode him around the perimeter of the camp, careful not to stir up too much dust. The others ceased their activities and watched me in silence.

The pinto had a soft mouth and responded easily to my tugs on the reins. I spurred him away from the camp and down a narrow trail, encouraging him into a gallop. The paint had good muscle, power, good reflexes. After several minutes together, he seemed to anticipate commands—turning, backing, slowing, speeding up—a half second before my pressure on the reins. The horse reacted as if he knew me.

I rode back into camp and dismounted in front of Chávez and Borrego. Borrego looked at me and nodded slightly, as if in grudging acknowledgment of my ability to ride, spat on the ground, then turned and walked away.

Chávez stepped forward and said, "Bueno, let's eat!"

Chávez strode over to the stew pot where the others had already gathered. I followed. After the men had been served, El Enano handed me a chipped, red clay bowl of an odd-smelling concoction, which I consumed using my fingers and by tilting the vessel up to my mouth. Whether swayed by hunger borne of the long walk or the desire to belong, the stew tasted good to me. El Enano beamed as he watched me eat, nodding his approval.

Dark, rich coffee accompanied the stew, a savory brew laced with sugar and the milk of *el chivo*, the goat. No sooner had I returned the bowl and wiped my fingers on my pantalones when Chávez gave the order to mount.

El Enano sidled over to me and whispered, "We ride to the camp of the vaqueros who attacked the villages of San Blas and Gallegos. They burned the corn, took the stores of food, and whipped the men they caught in the fields. One was beaten to death. They dragged two young girls into the church where they were raped by all ten men. When they rode away, they took the two young girls with them."

I thought of San Lorenzo—the village, the people, gone.

I looked at the riders, all hurrying to untie their caballos. My heart hammering, I hastened to the picket line to saddle the paint. As I was cinching up the rig, Chávez materialized before me, holding out a leather cartridge belt stuffed with bullets and an attached holster nesting a heavy Colt .45 caliber revolver.

"Can you use this?" he asked.

"*Sí*, I can."

I strapped on the wide belt, settled the holster, then deftly reversed it to accommodate my left-handedness. Chávez smiled his approval.

"Ah, *el siniestro*!" he said.

El siniestro. The left hand. But the word had other meanings—sinister, ominous, disaster, and fire. I adjusted the belt until the holstered pistol rode comfortably on my hip. Borrowing the necessary items, I cleaned and oiled the revolver and loaded the chamber.

El Enano poured water over the campfire, the hissing sound carrying through the evening air.

Before mounting, each of the riders approached El Enano, removed the dwarf's large sombrero, and rubbed his knobby head. I held back, unsure. As each of the men conducted the ritual, El Enano looked at me and pronounced their names—Sánchez, Borrego, Jaramillo, Olguín, Herrera, and lastly, Chávez.

After taking his turn, Chávez turned to me and said, "To rub the *cabeza* of one such as El Enano brings good luck."

The riders watched as I stepped forward and stroked the dwarf's head.

"How do I call you?" asked El Enano.

Before I could answer, Chávez called out, "He is Carlos del Santiago," surprising me with the new name.

"Very well, then," said the dwarf. He looked around at the gathered Indios, smiled, and announced, "Del Santiago."

Before I stepped away, the little man clasped my right forearm tightly, looked me hard in the eyes, and said, "You are going to do well this ride, amigo. I know it in my heart."

Then, he turned and mounted a stocky dun, using a stump to reach the stirrups.

Glancing around to make certain all were ready, Chávez commanded, "*Vámanos*." Let's go.

The timbre of his diaphragm-seated voice echoed off the granite walls. Eight of us, including El Enano, followed Chávez single file down the trail. Not knowing what to expect, I brought up the rear and regarded the others. The mood was somber, quiet. All rode with their eyes focused straight ahead, the only sounds the clopping of hooves and the jingling of tack.

Some were smiling.

The Ears

Las Orejas

The next morning, only minutes past sunrise, found us riding down a thickly wooded slope toward a sandy plain. I could tell by gestures exchanged between Chávez, Borrego, and Sánchez, who rode at the front of the column, that the quarry had been spotted. We rode out of the concealment of the trees and onto the flat, where we formed a rank of riders eight abreast.

Alone with my fear and nervousness, I rode in the middle of the line next to Chávez. The men we trailed were about eighty yards away, watering themselves and their horses at a shallow creek. There were ten of them. It appeared as though they were preparing to abandon their makeshift camp. Save for the two captives, none were mounted. Their pistol belts and bandoleras hung from the limbs of a mesquite tree, their rifles stacked against the trunk or scabbarded.

The vaqueros laughed and joked. One pissed in the stream. The girls taken from the village of Gallegos were each tied on a horse, their ankles bound to the stirrups with leather straps, their wrists lashed to the wide, round saddle horns. Neither of them could have been more than twelve years old.

A vaquero reached up and fondled one of the girl's small breasts. When she jerked away, he slapped her across the face. She hurled a curse at her attacker. We watched as he leaped onto the horse behind her and tore away her dress.

I looked over at Chávez. His mouth, set in a tight line, made the muscles in his jaw ripple. I glanced at the others. They held their revolvers and rifles, impatient, waiting for Chávez to give the order to attack.

Fear and nervousness departed as if on wings. I slid the .45 from its holster and hefted it. It felt good. I knew men would die in the next few minutes. I knew I could be one of them.

Nine vaqueros stood near the bank of the creek, looking away, the tenth still on horseback, intent on the girl. Chávez spurred his black and it surged forward, the rest of us falling in alongside and slightly behind, charging in a wide line with plenty of space in between. The strong paint manifested a smooth, controlled gallop. I gave him his head and let him carry me.

All sound ceased save for the harsh pounding of the horses, a thundering that vibrated the crust of the earth. The sound overpowered me, yet the vaqueros had taken no notice of our attack.

I rode low on the neck of the pinto, leveling the revolver, extending my left arm in an attempt to aim. I had never shot a gun from horseback.

I had never shot anyone, but now did not doubt that I could. During those few closing seconds, I knew I could pull the trigger. I knew I wanted to.

When we were forty yards way, the vaqueros heard us and wheeled around, staring in surprise. The one with the girl leaped to the ground and raced toward the weapons.

While the vaqueros reached for revolvers and rifles, we opened fire. Two went down immediately and two more ran toward the girls, intent on using them as shields, but Herrera shot them. An errant bullet went into the chest of a steel gray horse and it dropped, flailing and screaming.

They scrambled toward their horses and tried to mount. The caballos, sensitive to the sudden frightened reaction of their riders, tensed and shied, making them difficult to control.

One vaquero stood in the open, directly in front of us, and fired his revolver repeatedly at Chávez, each bullet miraculously missing its mark. Without checking his speed, Chávez ran the man down, the impact of the black horse knocking him several feet. Skidding the gelding to a stop, Chávez spun the caballo and rode back to the writhing vaquero. He fired three bullets into the man's chest, then reined back to the fray.

The dust and sand, stirred by the wind, the milling horses, and the running men, hung thick in the air. Refracting the late afternoon sunlight, it took on a pastel hue and drifted slowly, opaque. Dreamlike, I rode through the yellow cloud.

It was over in seconds, all ten vaqueros down, seven dead, the girls unharmed. Borrego suffered a slight flesh wound to his thigh. Sánchez's horse took a bullet in the stomach and had to be dispatched. While El Enano and Jaramillo cut the captives loose, the others rifled through the pockets of the dead, finding a few pesos, a pocketknife. Herrera and Borrego cut the ears from the men they killed and compared them. Chávez walked up to one of the wounded men and shot him through the right eye. The back of the skull blew apart. Shards of bone, clumps of hair, blood, and brains scattered in the dust.

Still mounted, breathing hard, I held my revolver. Several yards in front of me one of the wounded vaqueros rolled over and pulled a *pistola* from a back-mounted holster. Struggling to a kneeling position, he took slow, deliberate aim at Herrera's back, only ten feet way.

Shots sounded—once, twice, a third time—in rapid succession and the vaquero flopped to the ground, bullets in the shoulder, chest, and head. When my pinto ceased his nervous dancing, I realized my revolver was smoking, that it was I who had fired. That it was I who had killed.

Herrera, wide-eyed, looked at the dead man, then at me. His dark face illuminated with a wide grin followed by a burst of laughter.

"Well done," he said.

He strode over, sliced off the dead man's ears, and brought them to me. As he placed the bloody objects in my right hand, he narrowed his eyes and whispered, "*Gracias*."

• • •

I walked among the dead. Spotting a rifle lying in the dirt, I picked it up and ratcheted the lever, ejecting an unspent cartridge. A .30-30, a well-cared-for Winchester Model 94, scratched and dirty but serviceable. I glanced at the other riders, but no one else seemed interested in claiming it, so I took the weapon along with a shell-filled bandolera that was draped across an adjacent body.

On the way back to my pinto, I stopped next to three dead men lying side by side. Two had discernible bullet wounds in the chest and abdomen, but there was little blood, only fist-sized crimson stains on their camisas.

Beneath the third body, a wide puddle of blood had flowed from the victim and thickened, drawing hundreds of flies. I wondered how so much blood could have come from this man, yet the others spilled less than a cupful each.

As I pondered the difference, I looked up to see Herrera approaching. In contrast with the others, Herrera took pride in his dress and hygiene. He was bothered by the least amount of dust or grime on his garb or skin and took pains to remove it. Herrera shaved every day, carefully trimming and shaping his thick moustache. Whenever we camped near a stream, he washed his clothes and laid them across rocks or tree limbs to dry. He was always grinning, laughing. In a band of fighters, warriors, Herrera stood out, his appetite and his passion for killing unsurpassed by any. He was most happy when he was on the trail, on the hunt for men to kill. Once he told me his dreams were filled with images of himself riding on a giant steed through a large cluster of vaqueros and hacendados, shooting them down one by one.

Herrera walked up to me, stood for a moment looking down at the pool of blood, and said, "Artery."

• • •

Two miles upstream from the scene of the fight we made camp for the night. El Enano cooked a stew made from birds Sánchez shot, creek water, salt, wild onions, and some chiles. It smelled delicious, but I could not eat. I watched as the little man tended the girls' rope burns and scratches, as Chávez took them some stew. I knew we would return them to Gallegos unharmed.

• • •

After tending to our horses, our wounds, and our weapons, we laid next to the campfire tending to our own private thoughts.

Sánchez wondered aloud about his family in Ciudad Chihuahua many miles to the east: his three children, his pregnant wife. Borrego wondered about his brother who he believed had joined the hacendados' mercenary forces. Jaramillo, the oldest of the band, wondered if he would ever see his grandchildren again. He spoke of his wife whom he had buried ten years earlier. Olguín wondered where we would find decent graze and corn for the horses.

Herrera, still smiling from the fight, wondered when we would reach the next town where liquor and women could be found. Spinning the chamber on his revolver, he also wondered when he would get to kill again.

New to the land and the people, not proficient with their mountain dialect, I said nothing, only listened. But I wondered if I would live to see twenty years of age.

• • •

I slept little that night, the sounds of charging horses and gunfire filling my dreams. Several times I woke with a start and reached for my revolver. Each time it took long minutes for my heartbeat to slow down as I heard only the crickets and the night birds.

When I rose at daybreak, I found I was still clutching the drying, blood-scabbed ears in my right hand.

Dying Men

Los Hombres Moribundos

Four days after returning the young girls to their families we were still on the trail. Hunger and thirst had turned both horses and riders lean and edgy. The men were sullen and seldom spoke. Hot sun, parched air, blistering wind, and dense, irritating dust turned our throats so dry it was hard to speak or spit out the still-biting taste of gunpowder and smoke.

I didn't remember much about the fight except that it was over in only a few heartbeats. When I was alone I smelled sulfur and sweat and the warm, coppery odor of fresh blood. I heard the cries of the fighting and the dying, both the hunters and the hunted, both men and horses. In moments of battle they sounded alike.

The image of the vaquero I killed, the crimson paste of hair and bone and brain sprayed across the ground, would not go away.

It woke me at night, shivering, glancing about frightfully, not sure where I was.

Men did not die like I thought they would, like I had read about in novels. They screamed.

They called out for their mothers.

The Night of Thunder and Fire

La Noche del Trueno y Fuego

The waxing moon finally appeared behind skittering gray clouds. The campfire suffered from a lack of dry wood as we sought warmth and slumber in our ragged blankets, serapes, and ponchos. Borrego, squatting by the embers, dumped the coffee grounds from his cup into the ashes and called for El Enano to come over and sit close.

We gathered around to watch and listen, smelling smoky from the fire, smelling of sweat, of horses, leather, and of gun oil. Sánchez and I stood side by side just within the fading light of the fire. Save for me, Sánchez was the youngest, and the most unlikely looking member of the band. I believed Sánchez was half Mexican and half Anglo, though I never asked and he never spoke about himself. He had eyes that suggested a tale of sadness, perhaps loss. Loss seemed to be a theme common among these men. The skin on his almost feminine face was soft, smooth, and he had a small wisp of a moustache that belied the fierceness he displayed in battle. His frame was thin, almost delicate, yet he worked and fought with power and poise, moving quietly in soft moccasins as if he were walking on air. Sometimes during quiet periods in camp, Sánchez pulled out a pencil stub, sharpened it, and wrote with a slow and deliberate concentration in a small, scarred, leather-bound journal. Once, I asked El Enano what he was writing and he replied, "Poetry."

Spitting onto the sandy ground, Borrego pointed to the glob of saliva and asked his companion to read it. El Enano, a brujo—a sorcerer—stared at the thin, silvery layer of spit and grew entranced as the moisture slowly seeped into the porous, sandy soil.

Somewhere far off, a wolf howled, then stopped suddenly. Night birds called intermittently and crickets chirped, then stilled. A thin cloud covered the partial moon and dulled the spit's reflection.

When the yellow moon reappeared, El Enano raised his gaze to Borrego and said, "Soon we will find them."

The dwarf peered intently down at the saliva again, then up at us, and said, "It will be a night of thunder and fire."

I moved away from the riders and sat on a rock, lost in my own thoughts, my head down between my knees.

Chávez walked over and sat down beside me. We sat together in silence for several minutes.

"Are you afraid?" he asked.

"No," I lied.

"Then you are a fool."

I started to respond, but he quieted me with a look.

"Risk is like sugar," he said. "Risk sweetens the fight, but fear is a gift. You must accept the fear, embrace it, let it work for you. He who has no fear dies early. Fear will help you read the risk correctly. Fear is often your ally."

Chávez looked up at the moon, then continued. "There is a place you must find within yourself, a place around which the fighting revolves. It is a core of the deepest silence, a stillness, even when all about you is madness and fighting. It is a center you must come to know and embrace. During the fighting, it is important for you to remain in that center. If you lose the center within you, if you lose that special balance, you will lose control. When you lose control, you will likely die."

"Are you afraid?" I asked. "Do you have fear?"

"Always," he replied.

"What are you afraid of?"

"I am afraid I will die before I kill them all."

• • •

The next morning we continued following the tracks of the horses—seventeen prize animals taken from the herd of Beltrán, Sánchez's uncle, along with seven shod ponies ridden by the thieves, vaqueros from Mueller's large rancho. For three days and nights we followed the tracks, gradually gaining on the animals and the men who had stolen them.

Nearing evening of the fourth day, thick, dark clouds appeared on the horizon, heavy condensations that loomed and threatened. Borne closer by high winds, the clouds rumbled, curled, and grew thicker, darker. Soon they obscured the sun and tiny drops of rain struck my face. Wrapped in my poncho, I pulled my sombrero down tightly and huddled close to the neck of my pony. Gusts of wind stirred and rattled the brush along the side of the trail. The biting wind howled across the ridgetops sounding like a thousand wolves.

Gilberto Candelaria, Beltrán's wrangler, had been scouting ahead. He rode out from the darkness and a curtain of rain toward us. Chávez spurred his black to meet him and they spoke quietly for several minutes. Wet and cold, we sat our horses and waited. Seconds later, Chávez turned in his saddle to face us.

Pointing in the direction from which Candelaria rode, he said, "They are camped two ridges away to the south, about four miles from here."

A clap of thunder punctuated his words. The wind gusted again.

"This night," he said, "when they have finished their meal, we will take them."

El Enano, hunched and shivering over his caballo next to me, looked up to the heavens, and said, "*Sí*, this will be a night of thunder and fire."

• • •

The rain had slacked somewhat as we squatted near the base of a low ridge, watching as Chávez slid down from his lookout position near the top. All eyes were on him as he said in a hushed voice, "There are seven of them. Two are guarding the horses that have been placed in an old rock corral a short distance away. Another is walking the perimeter of the camp as sentry. The remaining four are hunched around the fire, drinking and playing cards."

He searched each of our faces, then said, "We take them now!"

Chávez stepped over to where I was standing and asked, "Do you pray?"

"No," I replied.

"Pray now," he said.

I checked the loads in my rifle and revolver and secured the bandolera over my shoulders. I leaped onto my pinto, and the horse, sensing my nervous anticipation, turned into wild muscle between my knees, anxious to move, anxious for the fight.

Thunder rumbled and rolled overhead as we guided our mounts quietly to the ridgetop. Through the light rain, we could see the camp below. Barely illuminated by the glow of the dying fire, the horse thieves were preparing for sleep.

At the next burst of thunder, Chávez screamed an atavistic cry as our signal. As the rain started falling in dense sheets, we charged down the slope, firing into their midst. Flames from the tips of rifles and revolvers spat brief light into the growing darkness. Powder smoke stung my eyes, making tears that mixed with the rain that ran down my face onto my poncho.

Caught off-guard, the thieves scurried for their firearms and cover, pulling bullets from their cartridge belts and bandoleras as they ran, and trying to load chambers with cold fingers. Taking aim at a young bandit by the fire who was thumbing rounds into his revolver, I shot and was blinded by the smoking flash, my arm tingling from the recoil. Thunder boomed, vibrating off the adjacent walls of the sierra. *Relámpagos* shot from the heavens in jagged streaks, each strike illuminating the camp. I spurred my horse past the fallen boy, no more than fourteen years old, and saw I'd blown his head away.

El Enano, riding low on his dun, sped past me, firing over and over into the chest of one of the thieves. The man's coat exploded open, miniature wells of blood widening on his camisa as he collapsed to the ground.

Herrera shot two men during the initial charge, one bullet for each of them. He held tightly to his wheeling, frantic mount as he searched for others to kill.

I glanced sideways and saw Chávez riding past and firing his revolver, his obsidian eyes reflecting the lightning.

More thunder, more gunfire. It was over in little more than a minute. The cries of the wounded merged with the sounds of the rumbling sky and falling rain. Gooseflesh raised beneath my poncho.

The downpour drenched, then extinguished, the campfires. Clouds obscured a sliver of moon. Chávez examined each of the fallen—four dead, three dying. He placed the tip of his revolver to the heads of each of the wounded and pulled the trigger, the sound merging with the thunder. I watched, shivering from the cold, rain seeping into my open serape, wind curling around my legs, the smell of gunpowder and death hovering just above the ground.

Others went for Beltrán's caballos, but I only sat my pinto and stared at the dead with their open eyes and open mouths, rain washing into them. The thunder crashed once more, this time closer.

The fire flared with newfound dry wood that El Enano fed to the smoldering embers. Despite the rain, the flames blazed higher, turning into a funeral pyre, lighting the scene as thunder shook the landscape. One by one, the dead were piled onto the flames. The stench of burning flesh insulted the clean desert air, saturated it, contaminated it with ash and smoke and the oil of human carcasses.

• • •

By the time dawn broke over the eastern ridge, we were mounted. Ahead of us Beltrán's horses danced along the trail, eager to run. Ahead of the horses, storm clouds drifted, delivering occasional peals of thunder and parting just enough to allow scattered passage of the sun's rays. Behind us, near a ring of stones that once contained a fire, charred bone, boot leather, and bits of hair and cloth littered the washed-out, bloodied campsite.

Chávez reined up to me and we looked back.

"This place will be haunted now," he said. "Like all the others."

In the distance, thunder boomed a cannonade and I felt the low, rolling shudder of the earth beneath me.

The Message

El Recado

The only sound heard in camp was the screeching of the jays while they fought over scraps of food as the men busied themselves with the care of guns and gear. Lost in the smell of pines and spruce, sheep tallow, leather, and my own sweat, I rubbed the oil into the aged and cracked fenders of my saddle. The sudden eruption of a galloping horse made me look up in time to see old Jaramillo spurring his scrawny bay into the clearing. He gave a sharp whistle, the signal for danger.

Activity ceased as we hurried to the rider. Jaramillo sought out Chávez and told him, "Riders on the low road to Tascate, a dozen in all, perhaps thirty minutes away. It could be the same twelve vaqueros who were at Potrillo."

Potrillo. The vaqueros had come upon fifteen-year-old Teresa Gómez as she filled water buckets at the stream. The leader had grabbed her long black hair, dragged her into the nearby trees, and raped her. When he was finished, the others had taken their turns, then left her for dead. Her parents found her later that night and carried her home. Though badly beaten and bruised, she would live. Teresa said the riders called their leader Morales.

Chávez barked a command to saddle and bridle the caballos and check our weapons. We were ready and mounted in minutes.

"We ride to the place where the trail narrows between the black rocks and wait for them," said Chávez.

Pointing to El Enano and me, he continued, "You come with me."

Looking over at Borrego, Sánchez, Herrera, and Olguín, he instructed, "Hide in the rocks. When the vaqueros pass through, come up behind them, guns at the ready."

To Jaramillo he said, "You will lead the caballos into the trees where they will not be seen, then rejoin us."

• • •

As the twelve vaqueros steered their mounts through the constricted pass between the pocked lava boulders, they slowed, then halted, and stared at us standing in the trail—Chávez in the middle, El Enano on his right, and me to his left. The dwarf and I pointed our revolvers at the riders. Chávez's guns remained holstered, his sinewy arms loose at his side. His long hair ruffled in the slight breeze.

The trail just past the boulders widened enough for the riders to assume positions of four abreast, three rows deep. A tall vaquero in the front, second from the left, urged his horse forward two steps and stopped. Squinting, catlike eyes were set like crevices deep in his thin, angular face. His mouth, a sneering line, was edged with long black moustaches that hung past his sharp chin.

Chávez took a step forward and said, "We are looking for the men who violated the little girl at Potrillo two suns ago."

Cat-eyes chuckled, then erupted into raspy laughter. "And what do you intend to do with these men when you find them?" he asked, and spat onto the ground near Chávez's boots.

"We will see they never rape again," Chávez replied.

Cat-eyes grinned, his teeth yellow against the black moustache. "I see only three horseless men," he said. "One of them is only a *pinche gringo mozo*, and one a dwarf."

Sweeping an arm in the direction of his riders, Cat-eyes continued, "We are twelve. I am Efrén Morales, killer of men. I step on *insectos* and *piojos* like you every day."

He spat again, this time striking Chávez's boots, and said, "Do you think you can prevail against us?"

Without taking his eyes off Morales, Chávez clicked his tongue. In response, Herrera, Olguín, Sánchez, Borrego, and Jaramillo stepped out from behind the rocks, cocking revolvers and ratcheting rifle levers as they moved. The sounds crackled through the dry air. Each stood within five feet of a rider, each pointing his weapon at a chest or head. Herrera was grinning.

Morales assayed his predicament. His gaze returned to Chávez, and he spat again, this time the saliva landing with a loud splat on the Indian's pantalones.

Chávez took another step forward and said, "I am Chávez."

Morales stiffened in his saddle, his cat-eyes turning wary. "I have heard of you," he said. "Mostly lies, I think."

Looking around again, Morales leaned forward in his saddle and said, "I count only eight campesinos."

Glancing into the trees, then back at Chávez, he asked, "Are there more hiding in the rocks and trees like cowards, afraid to show themselves, afraid to face Morales?"

Bringing himself to full height in the saddle, Morales continued, "Besides, I don't think you have the cojones to shoot us."

Without moving, Chávez said, "Carlos, shoot the man on his right."

I fired the .45, sending a round through the right lung of the vaquero, the slug ripping open a hole in the chest and the impact knocking him off the horse. Startled by the report, horses reared and lunged, confused riders holding tight to reins as the animals danced around the badly wounded rider. Two vaqueros at the rear reached for pistolas, but Herrera and Borrego gunned them down. The rider on Morales's left pulled a rifle from its scabbard and El Enano shot him in the head.

Herrera fired at another vaquero, but the bullet struck the horse. Screaming, the wounded animal reared, bucked, and bolted from the milling cluster and charged back down the trail. As horse and rider flew past, Herrera shot the man out of the saddle. The fallen rider clawed at the wound to his shoulder and was trying to rise when Herrera walked over and fired a bullet into the back of his head.

The seven remaining riders settled their mounts.

"Raise your hands and place them on top of your sombreros and sit still," said Chávez. "The first to lower his hands will be shot."

Chávez had not moved from his position, nor had he drawn a revolver.

A foolish vaquero dropped his hand to pull a pistola when Herrera, standing no more than three feet away, sent a bullet through the middle of his face. Already dead, the vaquero tumbled from his horse, hitting the ground head first. The skull split open, making a sound like a smashed pumpkin.

Chávez addressed the six surviving horsemen, one of them Morales. "Dismount slowly. Once on the ground, place your hands on top of your heads."

El Enano, Sánchez, and Olguín watched the riders closely, anxious to shoot the first who violated the order. When all were on the ground, El Enano went from man to man removing pistolas and knives, placing some of them in his sash and throwing the rest into the brush.

Chávez looked over at me and said, "Make certain your man is dead."

I walked over to the prone form. I had seen Chávez and Herrera lay the tips of their revolvers against the skull and pull the trigger. I wondered how it would be. My hand shook, but by the time I reached the man, he was dead.

When Jaramillo brought our caballos, we mounted up. With each of us leading one or two of the riderless horses, we herded the horseless vaqueros, hands still on their heads, toward camp.

• • •

Morales, naked, hung from his wrists, his feet dangling two feet above the ground. The ropes that held him were looped over the thick limb of a large roble and tied off to a smaller tree. Several feet away, the five other vaqueros squatted, naked. Chávez had ordered them to remove their clothes and boots saying, "A naked man does not fight as well as one who is clothed."

Looking up at Morales, Chávez asked, "Did the Gómez girl bring you pleasure?"

Morales smiled boldly and said, "*Sí,* she fought hard. I like it when they fight like that. By the time we were finished with her, she wasn't fighting anymore."

He laughed. Then, with a hard, defiant look, he spat at Chávez, spraying his white camisa.

Ignoring the insult, Chávez turned to the naked vaqueros. "Who among you also violated the child?"

Nervous, the five men looked at one another and at Chávez, each of them shaking their heads and pleading innocence.

Morales burst into hoarse laughter and shouted, "All of them! All of them, save for Acosta! The *pendejo* Acosta was afraid and stood back saying Hail Marys over and over while we enjoyed the little *puta. ¡Mierda!* Acosta cried like a baby when she screamed. He is not much of a man, no?"

Chávez asked, "Which of you is Acosta?"

A slight young man rose, head bowed, his delicate hands covering his genitals.

Walking over to him, Chávez asked, "Who do you ride for, you and these men?"

Timidly, Acosta answered, "Señor Mueller."

"Did hacendado Mueller send you to Potrillo to commit this deed?"

"*Sí,*" Acosta replied. "He wanted us to scare the campesinos, to frighten them into leaving their land so he could move his cattle onto their fields."

Pointing to the other four vaqueros, Chávez asked, "Did these men have their way with the girl?"

Looking away, Acosta, barely audible, answered, "*Sí.*"

Chávez indicated the pile of clothes and boots and told Acosta to dress. He then ordered Borrego to burn the rest as the remaining vaqueros watched wide-eyed, knowing they would not leave this place alive.

When Acosta was clothed, Chávez said, "Reclaim your *caballo* from the remuda and saddle it. Before you leave this camp, however, you will witness the fate of your companions. Then, you will ride to the Mueller rancho and take him a message from me. You will tell Señor Mueller that for every campesino harmed by his vaqueros, Chávez will kill ten of his men."

Trembling, tears in his eyes, Acosta walked to the remuda. Borrego, Herrera, and I watched him, hands on our revolvers.

Chávez returned to where Morales swung from the ropes. He pulled his Mexican bowie knife from the sheath, the blade gleaming in the late afternoon sun. He ordered Borrego and Olguín to grab the vaquero's ankles and pull his legs apart. Chávez reached up, seized Morales's testicles in his left hand, and sliced them off.

As Morales screamed, jerking on the ropes, Chávez held out the bloody scrotum in his open hand to the four remaining naked vaqueros. The men squirmed, terror clouding their faces.

"This is what happens to men who rape my people," Chávez said. He threw the grisly trophy among them and the startled vaqueros squirmed and scooted away from the bloody cojones.

With another deft move, Chávez sliced off Morales's penis and dropped it in the dirt. Morales's screams reverberated off the canyon walls as blood from the wound poured out onto the ground. Borrego and Olguín released Morales's ankles and stepped back. I retreated into the lengthening shadows and tried to keep the gorge from rising in my throat. El Enano shuffled over, placing himself between me and the others.

One of the vaqueros jumped up and tried to run, but Herrera shot him in the knee. He walked over to the downed man, thrust the end of his revolver into his right eye, and was about to pull the trigger when Chávez stayed him. Thrashing on the ground, the vaquero's screams mingled with those of Morales.

Chávez watched Morales fight his ropes for a few minutes, then turned to Borrego, pointed to the wounded man, and said, "Bring me another vaquero." Herrera was disappointed at not being permitted to kill the man.

As Borrego and Olguín hung the wounded man up next to Morales, Chávez addressed us, saying, "The rest are yours."

Sánchez and Jaramillo began sharpening their knives on fine-grained sandstone rock.

• • •

An hour before dawn we packed up and rode out of camp. In the light of the high half-moon I could see the five men hanging from the roble. Two were dead, having bled their lives away. Morales and the others were still alive, but with no hope of surviving. Already the crows were gathering for the feast. When the sun rose, the vultures would arrive.

Few people ever traveled this trail, and it would be days before someone came upon the corpses.

Chávez rode in the lead. I rode in the middle, just behind Herrera. The only sounds were the clip-clopping of the caballos, the jingling of metal fittings, and the squeak of saddle leather. Though *compañeros* surrounded me, I had never felt so alone.

The Knife

El Cuchillo

As I untangled the knots in my pinto's mane, I felt a presence behind me. I turned to find Chávez standing only three feet away, his head tilted, his eyes perceptively narrowed, concerned, as though he was about to tell me something important. I stepped away from the caballo, faced him, and waited.

"You did not join in the cutting of Morales and the others," he said.

Though it was a statement, not a question, it was clear Chávez awaited an explanation.

How could I tell him I was revolted and sickened? How could I tell him that I did not have the stomach for such mutilations? How could I tell him the truth and not appear weak?

All of the riders carried at least one knife. The knives were used to carve meat or to cut leather. They were used in battle. At the fight in San Augustín, one of Herrera's revolvers ran out of bullets and the other jammed. Reholstering them, he unsheathed his knife, a twelve-inch fighting blade, rode up behind a foe, and plunged it into his back repeatedly, then threw the body to the ground. On another occasion, Herrera took a captive aside and slit his throat, nearly taking off the victim's head in the process.

Borrego and Olguín were also skilled knife fighters. Olguín once told me that any man who had felt the impact of a bullet and the cut of a knife would tell you he would much rather be shot than stabbed.

Chávez waited for my answer. He sensed my discomfort, but did not alter his gaze. I looked down at the tip of my boots, then back up at him, and said, "I have no knife."

Chávez turned and walked away. I did not know if I had been condemned as a coward because I had not fulfilled my role as one of the fighters, one of his warriors. I returned to my pinto's mane and began removing briars.

Minutes later Chávez reappeared. In his right hand was a sheathed knife, the scabbard fitted with a thick leather thong for wearing around one's neck. He handed it to me.

"Now," he said, "you have a knife." He patted my pinto on the rump and walked away.

I removed the knife from the sheath and examined it. As a child I wished for a hunting knife but was denied. My mother did not want such things in the house, and we had no money to purchase one anyway.

I turned the knife over and over in my hands. It was well used. The nicks and scars on the blade suggested it had seen many battles. A fighting knife, it had been fashioned from a British World War I bayonet, the blade shortened to seven and a half inches and honed razor-sharp. The original wooden handle had been well cared for and remained solidly riveted to the steel shank.

The knife felt good in my hand, the weight and balance comfortable. I knew the knife had taken many lives, and I wondered who the previous owners might have been.

Replacing the *cuchillo* in the sheath, I looped the thong around my neck, letting the weapon dangle on my chest in the manner of the indios. I wandered through the camp looking for Chávez. When I found him I nodded and said, "*Gracias.*"

He nodded back and said, "Fighting and killing with a knife requires that you close with your enemy. It is not like using a gun. With a knife you get close enough to touch him, to smell him. With a knife you can become stained with his blood as well as your own.

"Remember this, Carlos, because it brings you close to your foe, a knife is a far more intimate weapon than a gun. You, in turn, must become intimate with the knife, become used to her feel, her touch, her textures. Know what she is capable of accomplishing and respect her for it. A knife can get stuck in bone or gristle and can be difficult to withdraw. Bone can deflect the blade from a fatal target."

Leaning closer, Chávez continued, "Direct it to the soft parts, the stomach, the throat. That is the easiest way to kill with a knife."

He clasped my shoulder, then motioned me to go away.

• • •

I couldn't sleep. In the light of the moon and stars I stared at the knife, turning it over and over in my hands, considering its history. I had honed the blade for over an hour on borrowed Carborundum and stropped it smooth with a length of leather Borrego gave me. Satisfied that it was sharp enough, I returned it to the sheath, looped it around my neck, and lay down in search of slumber.

Throughout the night the same dream appeared countless times. It was not so much a dream as recollections that somehow escaped from a deep recess of my memory, recollections I thought were long buried, that I wanted lost. They were recollections stirred to life, uninvited, possessing unwanted vitality as a result of the gift of the knife.

I dreamed of the priest, Father Bohland, and of Damien Vetter. Then I dreamed of Morales.

For the third time I jolted awake, sweating, breathing heavily. All around me the camp was silent save for the distant hooting of an owl and the snoring of some of the riders. The moon was waxing, just beyond half. I felt for the knife, found it hanging from my neck, and held it close for comfort.

The Watchman

El Vigilante

I never knew where Chávez came from. He never said. I never asked. It was said he was Yaqui, or Quechua, or Otomi, or Aztec, or even Apache. I heard he had eaten the hearts and flesh of men he had slain.

Whoever Chávez was, the torture, rape, and murder of his family had turned him into a warrior, a finely tuned fighter. Dedicated to righting wrongs, exacting justice, and conducting revenge wherever he saw it was needed, he was a vengeance-possessed wraith. Herrera said Chávez's passion for revenge exceeded his passion for food, for fine horses, for women. Herrera said Chávez's need for vengeance even exceeded his own immense passion for killing. In other lands in other times, Chávez would have been Robin Hood or Jesse James, men who fought against the rich and powerful, men who fought for the poor and the persecuted.

Chávez's white cotton camisa was usually stained with blood, and he wore his pantalones, the garb of the peasants, tucked into aged, worn, knee-high riding boots. Loaded bandoleras crisscrossed his chest in the pattern of an angled crucifix. Two vintage Colt .45s rested in well-oiled holsters that rode his hips, holsters that hung from a wide leather belt that girded his rock-hard belly. A Mexican bowie knife was scabbarded at his back and a fighting dirk was sheathed on the outside of his right boot.

His horse, black as death, was called Pesadilla—Nightmare. Chávez rode Pesadilla as if the two were one. As a horseman, he had no peer.

Chávez's eyes, hooded like those of a hunting hawk, blazed from beneath a battered felt sombrero, one I heard had been worn by his father who rode and fought beside the revolutionary leader Pancho Villa. His eyes, black as obsidian, seared, probed, darted, and danced.

Those eyes, like weapons, searched out and found men who tried to hide. Those eyes cut right into a man's soul.

Those eyes had seen great pain.

Sometimes at night Chávez would disappear into the canyons. Borrego told me the leader wished to be alone with his thoughts, to be alone to speak with the spirits of his dead wife and children. Darkness had become Chávez's smooth companion.

El Enano told me that God rode with Chávez, that He guided his warrior soul to smite those who would take the land of his people, their cattle, their fields, those who would torture, rape, and kill *los innocentes.*

But Chávez himself told me there was no God in Mexico, only churches and priests. That is why, he claimed, our time was taken up with fighting the devil. He became a watchman, a *vigilante,* for his people.

Only death, Chávez claimed, would keep him from fighting.

At first Chávez frightened me. I thought he might despise me, a gringo youth who presumed to fight alongside him. Instead, he embraced me, showed me his way. He instilled in me a love for the campesinos, a love for the land, the mountains, the desert. He instilled in me his sense of sierran justice. Justice, Chávez once told me, was something one had to fight for because it was seldom offered.

"The law is never on our side," he said. "The law is on the side of those who can pay for it. Those who pay for the law call it justice, but those who cannot afford it know that law and justice are not the same."

Chávez taught me his right and wrong. He taught me how to fight for the honor and dignity of the poor.

Chávez taught me how to kill.

Gringos my age wanted to be like their favorite baseball players or cowboys. I only wanted to be like Chávez.

I found myself walking like Chávez. I sat my caballo as he sat his, straight, head high, eyes always searching. I grew my hair long until it flowed out from under my sombrero like Chávez.

Chávez seldom spoke; thus I likewise remained silent. Once, though, I heard him sing. He admitted it was a song his mother sang to him. I have never forgotten the melody of the song or the timbre of his voice.

Like the others, I came to believe that God rode with Chávez.

I never stopped believing.

The Rattlesnake

El Cascabel

The stooped, wrinkled peon carried a superbly crafted homemade guitar. He stepped off the trail to make room for us as we rode past. He, with his snow-white hair and sparse chin whiskers, twinkling eyes, and gummy smile, waved as the horses jingle-clopped by him.

"*Buen viaje,*" he said, grinning. Good journey.

I reined my paint up next to him and asked, "Do you know the words to the song 'El Cascabel'? Can you play it?"

He nodded, sat down on a fallen juniper, and with deft, supple fingers plucked the cat-gut strings, his frail voice quavering, sometimes fading, sometimes rising. Chávez turned and rode back to listen.

When the old man finished the folk tune, I thanked him. Chávez tossed him a gold piece in a rattlesnake-quick movement and said, "That was the finest rendition of 'El Cascabel' I have ever heard."

The cascabel. The word could mean rattlesnake, but it was also used to describe a very happy person, such as the old man.

When we reached the village of San Martin, la gente stood at the edges of the streets, wary at our approach. As we rode into the town, a woman carrying a baby broke from the crowd and trotted alongside Pesadilla, telling Chávez, "We thought you were the Hinojosa gang returning. Three dead. Yesterday. So many tortured and robbed. Four raped, all the money from the cantina and the churches taken."

Chávez reined his caballo to a halt and looked down at her as she continued, breathless, "When they finished, they rode away into the hills from which you came."

Leaning over, Chávez placed a calming hand on her shoulder and said, "We are only here to gather a string of fresh horses. We intend no harm."

As we rode through the village in the late afternoon sunlight, men were preparing to fight in the plaza, and a small crowd had gathered to watch the contests. Two young men, donning tattered boxing gloves, were only moments away from a match. I spurred my pinto ahead to overtake Chávez.

"I want to fight," I said.

He shook his head. "The horses are more important."

I held my caballo in check until the rest of the riders had passed by, then I brought up the rear of the line.

• • •

The following dawn we rode back up the trail herding a dozen bays, *grullas*, roans, and pintos. Around midmorning we passed the place where the beaming old man played and sang "El Cascabel."

As Chávez rode past the fallen log, he said again to no one in particular, "That was the finest rendition of 'El Cascabel' I have ever heard."

We rode on another mile, and another, and another, and then we found him. He had been crucified upside down on a dead roble, his throat cut, the last of his blood pattering droplets on the ground and the leaves, the once beautiful guitar smashed to pieces at the base of the tree. A pair of crows perched on a nearby limb regarded us.

We reined up, staring, the minutes of silence broken only by the sound of the blowing, stamping horses and the flies worrying the body. Borrego made the sign of the cross several times. El Enano muttered a prayer in his Indian dialect. Chávez dismounted and walked over to the tree.

His eyes hard, Chávez regarded the dead man. He searched his pockets but did not find the gold piece. He stepped back a pace and studied the inverted sacrifice, the black flies crawling in and out of the mouth. He touched the shattered guitar with the toe of his boot.

Chávez looked up at me, his eyes the eyes of a rattlesnake, and said, "That was the finest rendition of 'El Cascabel' I have ever heard."

With a nod, he indicated that the old man be cut down and buried. El Enano, Sánchez, and I finished the chore without saying a word.

When it was done, we were washing our hands in a shallow creek when El Enano whispered, "It has been said that Jesus Christ, as a child, had nightmares about crosses."

• • •

In the small town of Trujillo we penned the caballos, washed the dust from our hands and faces at the plaza well, and walked over to the only cantina for tequila and food. Herrera murmured that he also hoped for love, his appraising eyes darting from one comely señorita to another.

Seated at a table in the dim candlelight was the bandit called Hinojosa. Surrounded by his gang, he was laughing, singing along with the small band, drinking pulque and sotol, touching the whores that hovered nearby, and telling obscene jokes about the old man he had crucified on the road beyond the town.

Chávez, his jaw clenched, squinted in the dark, his rattlesnake eyes crisscrossing the room until he found Hinojosa.

Spurs jingling, Chávez strode straight-backed past the large round table without looking at its occupants, approached the band, and requested a song.

As the guitar player strummed the opening chords and rhythm of "El Cascabel," Chávez turned and walked over to the table to stand before Hinojosa. The outlaw twirled a gold piece in his long fingers. The music crescendoed. Hinojosa sat silent, sullen, eyeing Chávez.

When the band fluidly entered the second chorus, Chávez snatched his revolver from its holster and fired a bullet into the middle of Hinojosa's forehead. The bandit crashed backward onto the floor, blood seeping from a gaping hole in the back of his head.

Hinojosa's riders jerked toward their guns, but ours were already drawn, hammers cocked, the barrels pointed at their heads. Chávez stared at them each in turn as the musicians neared the end of the song, daring them to try. Stooping, he pried the gold piece from the dead man's hand, turned toward the band, and tossed it to the *guitarrista*.

"That," he said, "was the second-best rendition of 'El Cascabel' I have ever heard."

The Grave

La Sepultura

Bright sun beat down, heating my flesh. Sweat was ephemeral. The desert plants, hardy and tough, wilted from the onslaught. The same heat cooked the rocks and soil beneath the hooves of my caballo, which plodded haltingly forward, head down with exhaustion and thirst.

I was the only gringo in the long, single file of riders as we passed through the now-deserted pueblo. Just beyond a low rock wall, a few paces from the road, was the campo santo. Near the wall was a fresh grave with a marker, laboriously cut and shaped from native sandstone, painstakingly inscribed by a loving hand. The marker bore the name Enrique Villareal.

I remembered him. He was among those who had resisted at the fight at Puente Salazar the week before. I remembered him slashing at me with his rusted machete, trying to behead me as I dodged and twisted and desperately tried to reload my revolver.

I remembered the shots that rang out from behind me and the dark blood exploding from the openings in Enrique's chest, throat, and head, blood that sprayed my shirtfront and face.

In those few slow motion seconds, I heard the sound of blood, the startling vibration of the fluid leaving his body in a great gush, forced out by the final beats of the heart. I heard the splattering of individual droplets as they struck the ground. Enrique's eyes, drained of color, tried to focus on me, pleading.

Then he fell.

I remembered turning and seeing Chávez, gun in hand, smoke swirling skyward from the barrel, a smile on his face.

The Brother

El Hermano

It was not as much a battle as it was a massacre. They had little chance against us: five dead, three wounded, two escaping across the midnight-colored basaltic ridge to the south to inform others that Chávez rides.

• • •

The ten armed vaqueros from the Mueller rancho had ridden into the tiny riverside pueblo of Hidalgo at dawn three days earlier, their caballos trampling the gardens of corn, beans, squash, and chiles.

The young men were gone to hunt for peyote. Most of the old men who remained in the village were beaten to death or shot. An old woman, a curandera, was ridden down and left in the dust of the road with a broken leg. Young girls, one only twelve years old, were raped repeatedly and left bleeding. The low-roofed houses constructed from river cane, ocotillo, and wood were fired and burned to the ground.

The evening after the attack, two nine-year-old boys mounted on a donkey rode into Chávez's camp and told us what had happened. We all listened in silence—Chávez, Herrera, Olguín, Sánchez, Borrego, El Enano, Jaramillo, and I. At the mention of the Mueller vaqueros, Borrego stiffened but said nothing.

Weary from long hours on the trail and lack of sleep, we rode into the village the following morning. Chávez dismounted and conferred with a surviving village elder as we watered our horses at the plaza well. We waited, feeling the summer heat creep across the dry ground and seep unrelentingly into our clothes and flesh. Flies buzzed around us but we ignored them. All of us watched Chávez, Borrego watching more intently than the rest.

When Chávez finished speaking with the old man, he wheeled around and strode to Pesadilla, leaped into the saddle, and turned to us, a hard, vengeance-black look in his eyes.

"We ride," he said.

• • •

We were in the saddle all day, stopping only for water and to allow the horses a few precious minutes to graze. Mounted again, we ate cold tortillas de maíz as the miles passed beneath us. Chávez passed around a roasted leg of goat provided by the villagers. Repeatedly, we checked the loads in our weapons and wiped the trail dust from our revolvers and rifles.

• • •

The vaqueros were not expecting pursuit and never heard us coming. They had stopped near the bank of the Río Colmillo and turned their unsaddled horses loose to graze on the lush grasses of the floodplain. Their rifles remained snugged in saddle scabbards; their gun belts hung on tree limbs.

Laughing, joking, even singing *cantos* under the shade of an álamo, they were unaware of our approach until we were within fifty yards.

For them, it was too late.

With an earsplitting cry, Chávez, firing two revolvers as he charged, led us into their midst. As the vaqueros dashed toward their horses, toward their weapons, toward cover, we swarmed over them like maddened wasps, firing, clubbing, slashing, trampling. Borrego, revolver raised, searched the faces of our quarry.

One of the vaqueros, wearing shiny black cavalry boots and a yellow bandanna around his neck, turned to fight. He waved a dagger above his head, daring me to take him. Unwilling to slow my mount, I rode him down, firing into his torso as I passed.

Suddenly, I went down, my pinto shot out from under me. Slamming against the ground, knocked breathless and blinded by the raised dust, I groped for my dropped revolver. Finding it, I peered through the dense fog of powdery earth and gun smoke looking for a target.

As the haze parted, I saw a vaquero striding toward me, rifle in hand. When he was within ten feet I fired off the remaining three rounds in my revolver. Two of the bullets struck—one in the groin, one in the chest—and he fell, kicking and swearing. Then he was dead.

With my revolver empty, I sought my rifle, but it was pinned under the fallen caballo. I picked up the dead man's rifle, levered it once, and saw that it, too, had no shells. As I looked around for another fallen weapon, a second vaquero ran toward me through the swirling yellow dust, a long knife in his right hand.

When he dashed in, trying to disembowel me with a swipe of the knife, I parried his move with a chop from the rifle. Recovering, he stepped back and regarded me as a snake would regard a mouse. I grabbed the rifle by the barrel, intent on using it as a club.

Again he lunged. I stepped aside to evade the strike and swung the rifle hard, missing his head by a scant inch. Before I recovered, he sliced again, cutting me on my right forearm, drawing blood.

The rifle proved too heavy and unwieldy for close-in fighting. I threw it to the ground and drew my cuchillo from the chest scabbard. Like being in the ring again, two men as equals, this was better.

The vaquero executed a straight-on stab at my chest that I evaded with a slight twisting and bending of my torso. I countered with a backhand clubbing of his forehead with the handle of the cuchillo.

Stepping back to collect his composure, the vaquero studied me for a second. Grinning through rotted teeth and an untrimmed moustache, he said, "Do you want to die, *cabrón*?"

Remembering the time Damien Vetter asked me the same question, I smiled back and felt a twinge of exhilaration.

Barely perceiving the sounds and movement of the fight around me, I stood in my calm center, content that I was in control. The vaquero took a long step toward me, lunging with the knife, his movements coming to me in slow motion. I watched the knife as it sliced past my chest, even saw droplets of my own blood on the blade from his earlier strike.

With his arm completely extended from the lunge, I brought my own blade straight up with all my strength, plunging it through his right bicep clear to the hilt. The force of the strike nearly broke his arm and he released his knife.

I yanked out the cuchillo and stepped away, ready to strike again, but it proved unnecessary. Blood from a severed artery spewed out, a black-crimson stream we both watched. The vaquero turned to look at me, the color of his face fading from copper to white. His blood, and his life, drained away into the sand and he collapsed.

In minutes it was over. Dense gun smoke and dust settled onto the scarred desert ground. Two of the vaqueros reached their caballos and galloped away. Startled from my trance, I caught a riderless horse and leaped onto it. I signaled to Sánchez, and together we started after the pair, but Chávez called out for us to return.

He explained, "They will tell the others of what happened here. They will tell hacendado Mueller that Chávez rides."

Five vaqueros were dead. Herrera and Borrego sliced the ears from the heads, still moist with blood. They strung them onto leather thongs to accompany a dozen more shriveled *orejas* from previous fights and hung them from their necks. Herrera's string of ears—black and stiff near the middle, rosy and soft close to the edges—swung low, touching his belt buckle.

Chávez bent over a wounded vaquero and fired a bullet into his right eye. He moved to the other and repeated the execution. On his way to the third, he paused near where I stood, revolver still in hand, pointed to my downed pinto, and said, "Take care of your *caballo*."

Dreading the outcome, I strode to my mount that lay near the edge of the battleground. He had two bullet wounds in his chest and another in the left flank. Kicking his hind legs, he tried to rise but could not. My rifle was still in the scabbard beneath him.

I borrowed one of Herrera's revolvers and with a prayerful sigh shot the pinto beneath the left ear. With the help of El Enano, I stripped off my saddle and bridle, retrieved the rifle, and went in search of my own revolver.

After cleaning the sand and dust from my weapons, I reloaded them. This done, I walked over to the man I had killed with the knife. I checked the pockets of his pantalones for pesos, but there were none. I probed in the pockets of his jacket and found nothing but a ragged-edged photograph. It was an image of the dead man. Seated on a bench, his arm around a beautiful woman, he was smiling. Four young children sat at their feet.

I wondered what his name was. I wondered what the woman and the children would do now. I placed the photograph into my own pocket.

• • •

Borrego, looking as if he were praying, knelt next to one of the eight killed. The dead man wore a yellow bandanna around his neck.

As we watched, Borrego lifted the man and, carrying him like a child, walked several yards into the sunshine and proceeded to excavate a shallow grave. When he finished, he laid the body within, covered it with the loose soil, then piled stones atop the mound. At the head of the grave, he laid out melon-sized rocks in the form of a crucifix. Standing silent, Borrego bowed his head, made the sign of the cross several times, then turned to rejoin us.

• • •

Bridle in hand, I walked among the dead vaqueros' grazing horses and picked out a steel gray gelding with darker gray spots splattered across his coat. He snorted at my approach and stepped away, ears flicked forward, eyes rolling. I spoke soothing words and reached out slowly, but the smell of blood and gun smoke spooked him backward and he skittered sideways. I felt the eyes of the other riders studying me.

It was the gray I wanted, no matter how long it took to catch him. My compañeros watched and waited in silence, holding on to the reins of their own horses. They stared when I finally placed my hand on the gray's shoulder, fitted the bridle over his head, and slipped the heavy Spanish bit into his mouth. They waited while I retrieved my saddle and threw it over the gray's back and tightened the cinch. They waited while I stood at the head of my pinto and gave thanks, while I knelt on one knee and cut a piece of his white mane and put it in my pocket with the photograph. They waited, grinning, when I stepped into the saddle. The gray was still for seconds, evaluating his new rider, then ducked his head and gave a few halfhearted crow-hops. Tiring of this, the caballo swiveled his large head around and tried to bite my booted foot. With one hand holding the reins and the other laying on his neck, I continued speaking softly to him for another minute. Then, together, we rode off.

* * *

Our silence was broken only by the sounds of the plodding horses, squeaking leather, and the clanking of metal fittings. The trail was wide enough for two mounts to walk side by side. I rode next to Sánchez, close enough to bump stirrups. I looked over at my ever-quiet companion, his dark face shaded by the wide straw sombrero. When he returned my gaze, I nodded toward Borrego, who rode directly in front of me and raised my eyebrows in silent question.

Sánchez leaned closer and whispered, "It was his brother."

The Vultures

Los Zopilotes

We had ridden over a mile from the battleground, heartbeats and breath finally beginning to slow, salty sweat still streaming down faces, arms, legs, and torsos, clothes smelling like gun smoke, bodies trembling from victory.

I grieved for my dead pinto, but the gray, half dancing as he walked, tossing his head, suited me fine. Shorter and stockier than the paint, this mountain-bred caballo would carry me to other adventures.

As we rode single file toward the east, I turned in the saddle to peer back down the trail behind us, beyond the low ridge just crossed.

Detecting dark, silent movement, I glanced upward at the sky and spotted a zopilote gliding in wide circles. Soon he was joined by another, then another, then more until dozens of the black vultures circled, descending in ever-tightening spirals toward the dead, seven of them lying where they fell on the sand in pools of their own blood. Borrego's brother, at least, was protected from the scavengers.

Come evening, the zopilotes would feast, but we would not. We rode to the next battle.

We rode to forget the one just past.

The Crow

El Cuervo

We had been riding for three days without stopping except to water the caballos and steal a bit of sleep when we came upon the three hanged men on the trail to Santa Isabel, three peones whose only crime seemed to be walking along the same trail ridden by hacendado Mueller and his vaqueros.

We had heard of the hangings while purchasing supplies in a pueblo to the south, and of Mueller's warning not to cut the dead men down. He had said he wanted them to serve as an example to others who would oppose him, interfere with him, or resist him.

It was close to sundown. On edge and tired from lack of sleep and meager rations, we sat our horses in silence and stared. The rotting corpses swayed in the slight breeze, the maguey riatas from which they hung squeaking against the rough-barked, thick limb of the spreading álamo. Ragged from hundreds of washings after being worn in the fields, faded camisas and pantalones dangled from the drying bodies, the cloying stench that followed each man at his death fouling the creosote-fragrant desert air.

A lone crow perched on the left shoulder of one of the dead men. Leaning across the face of the dark, stretched skin, *el cuervo* made several unsuccessful attempts to pluck out an eyeball. I pulled my revolver from the cracked leather holster, cocked it, and raised the weapon to fire a shot to frighten the black bird away.

Sánchez reached across the narrow space separating our caballos and placed a restraining hand on my arm.

Regarding me kindly, he said, “Crows have to eat too.”

The sun was sinking below the ridge behind the hanging tree. We rode on, our horses walking through the trio of elongated shadows stretched out across the trail.

Behind me, the crow called out, a trio of sharp, harsh notes that echoed across the wide valley.

The Devil

El Diablo

Days passed with no word of depredations by the hacendados' vaqueros. For a time, the tiny pueblos along the eastern flank of the Sierra Madres reveled in a kind of peace unknown for months.

We passed quiet time in camp, relieved to be off the trail and not having to endure the endless rides, the days on end of going hungry, and nights of little or no sleep. We hunted; we cleaned weapons. Nearly all smoked marijuana during idle times. We enjoyed each others' company.

Chávez remained silent. And restless. One morning as he saddled Pesadilla, he stated he was going into the mountains. He did not say when he would return. After he departed, others saddled their horses and rode off, some to their families, others with a need to be someplace else. Herrera, Sánchez, Jaramillo, and I stuck together and made plans to ride to Cuauhtémoc. I would look for a fight there, having missed the sport these past months. We would explore the cantinas and enjoy the diversions the town had to offer.

• • •

In the cantinas of Cuauhtémoc we wasted days and surrendered nights searching for love, for truth, searching for experiences of life. The old ones say you can't find truth in tequila and women, but maybe you can when you're chasing it with a passion you've never felt in a place you've never been.

In the taverns of the town we bloodied our fists on the faces of fortune. We counted our winnings and found we had lost.

We were trying to beat the devil, that we knew. We tried to sing our songs but found we didn't know the words.

The Adobe Wall

La Tapia

With our backs against the rough adobe wall, out of breath, nearly out of bullets, almost out of hope, and our horses too far away to reach, I wondered if we would ever ride again. I wondered why I was here. I wondered why I ever left Texas.

Sánchez, bleeding badly from a shoulder wound, swore softly and jammed shells into his revolver. Jaramillo, angry with himself because he had dropped his rifle during our flight, fired his revolvers blindly through the dense smoke of our own guns.

Why were these people shooting at us? Was it because of the horses we stole? Was it because of the twenty cows we took from hacendado Mueller's pasture? Was it because of the vaquero who worked for hacendado Mueller we shot and nailed to the trunk of a roble in the canyon?

Was it because we burned hacendado Terrazas's hacienda to the ground? Was it the fight we started at the cantina? Or was it because of the angry father of the beautiful señorita who took a shine to Herrera?

¿Quién sabe? Whatever it was, it cost us some blood. It would likely cost us some more.

"*Madre de Dios*," shouted Herrera as he fired his twin revolvers at the *soldados*. "We need to stay out of those goddamn cantinas."

The Guns

Las Armas

Herrera and I crouched in the shadows of a thorny mesquite just beyond hearing distance of a tiny pueblo. We were hungry. We'd had nothing to eat for four days except for wild onions and grapes and a small rabbit roasted over an oak fire. We tried to eat a dog Herrera shot, but it was old and stringy and made us sick. We thought about killing one of the horses and eating the meat, but that meant one of us would have to walk. Jaramillo had taken Sánchez home with him to treat his wounded shoulder.

We'd been sleeping on the rocky ground with only our serapes to ward off the night chill. When it rained, we simply leaned against the downwind side of the bole of a tree for a bit of protection. If there were no trees, we just got wet.

From behind the mesquite, Herrera's gaze remained riveted on a tienda located near the middle of the pueblo.

Grinning at me, he said, "We will obtain food there. And guns. We need guns."

He considered the tienda for another minute, and then said, "There are not many people around, and the few I see are not carrying weapons. This is going to be easy."

Tucking his ancient .45 into the waistband of his baggy canvas trousers, Herrera led the way through the midday heat into town, up the dusty street, and into the little store.

The *tendero*, an old, sun-darkened man, smiled as we entered. Politely, he offered his services.

"I am Gutiérrez," he said.

I started to reply but was interrupted when Herrera pulled the revolver from his pantalones and placed the end of the heavy steel barrel against the merchant's forehead.

"We need food," he told him.

When the tendero had filled two cloth sacks with coffee, beans, *masa*, posole, and a few tinned goods, Herrera instructed him to give all of the money to me. Pleading for mercy, his hands shaking, the old man took bills and coins from an old cigar box and placed them into my cupped palms.

Herrera, keeping the gun against the tendero's head, examined the used firearms arranged on a shelf behind the scarred wooden counter.

"For sale?" he inquired of Gutiérrez.

"*Sí*," the shopkeeper replied, confused.

While I counted the money and stuffed it into my pockets, Herrera ordered the shopkeeper to retrieve two slightly used .45 revolvers and a Winchester .30-30 along with accompanying ammunition.

When the weapons and bullets were piled onto the counter, Herrera, pointing at the arms, asked the tendero, "How much does this all come to?"

Sweating heavily, the merchant responded, "Around four hundred pesos, maybe five."

Turning to me, Herrera eyed the money bulge in my pocket and asked, "How much have we got?"

"About six hundred," I said.

"Pay this man for the guns and ammunition," Herrera commanded.

Surprised, I counted out the sum and laid it on the wooden planks that served as a counter.

Gathering the food, weapons, and boxes of ammunition, we fled out the door, down the street, and into the trees where we had tied our caballos.

• • •

Riding through the darkening barranca, I asked Herrera, "Why did you take the money and then use some of it to pay for the guns?"

"Stealing food is one thing," he said. "But stealing guns is dishonorable. One must pay for guns."

Spurring his caballo, Herrera cried, "*Vámanos*. It is time to find the others."

The Three Men

Los Tres Hombres

Borrego pulled a small *guitarra* from his saddlebag as El Enano commenced to play a mournful dirge on his fiddle. Sánchez and I dug the grave to the music, one large grave for the three men who dared take the daughter of Escobar.

• • •

We had come upon the trail of three of Mueller's vaqueros the morning following her kidnapping. From the tracks we could tell one of their horses was lame, tracks that were easy to pick out from among the many that had passed this way. We knew we would have them by nightfall. Escobar told us they were to be taken alive.

"If they have violated her," he said, "they are to be punished by me and no one else."

• • •

Chávez saw the body first, the young, beautiful, soft-skinned girl lying discarded alongside the trail. She had been beaten. Bruised and bloodied, her teeth were broken and her skull had been crushed. Blood still seeped from under her torn fingernails, evidence that she had tried to fight them off. She had been a pretty child, a lovely young woman, but no more.

While we remained astride our mounts, Escobar wrapped his daughter in his serape and asked Olguín to carry her back to her mother.

Looking up at us, five in all, his eyes moist, his voice as hard and jagged as flint, Escobar said only, "*Vámanos*."

We rode single file down the trail, Escobar in the lead, Chávez behind him, and the rest of us following in line.

We did not stop to eat, only to rest and water the caballos. As the sun, dirt-colored from a dust storm, began its descent toward the shadowed sierran ridge, we found the lame horse, abandoned and grazing along the bank of the Río Guajalote. Chávez and Escobar dismounted and examined the tracks nearby. Chávez indicated with his hands that two men were riding one mount, another riding solo.

Squatting close to the ground, Escobar silently studied the prints for a long time, touching the edges and rubbing the sand between his fingers. He rose but did not look at us this time. His gaze was fixed on the trail ahead.

From his caballo, Chávez, an expert tracker, regarded the impressions and determined the riders had passed this point two to four hours earlier.

Escobar broke the silence. "It will not be long," he said.

We rode along the narrow, winding trail from the highlands down and across the bajada to the Llano del Muerte—The Plain of Death—a wide, waterless, red sand and gravel expanse stretching westward to the horizon. The llano was known to have claimed men and horses alike.

As we rode we checked our canteens and glanced nervously at one another and at Escobar. Silent and brooding in the lead, he rode straight in the saddle, staring directly ahead and scanning the plains, searching, ever searching, for movement.

Moments later we spotted them a mile or more out on the llano. One man was riding a dun and two were doubled up on a roan, both horses tired and dragging their hooves in the dust. Escobar spurred his long-legged paint into a double-pace trot and followed the trail as it wound down out of the bajada, straightened out, and stretched across the flat llano.

Escobar urged his mount into a lope the animal could have sustained for miles without tiring. We fell in behind him, the hooves of our horses striking the ground at exactly the same time as his. The sharp, rhythmic sound vibrated the landscape, causing our quarry to turn and stare. As we closed in on them, the fleeing men tried desperately to spur their exhausted mounts to greater speed, but to no avail.

As we rode, two of us pulled revolvers from holsters and checked the loads, and two more yanked rifles from scabbards and chambered shells, the ratcheting mechanisms of the weapons sounding sharply above the noise of the pounding hoof beats. Now only four hundred yards separated us from the killers of Escobar's daughter. We increased our pace to a hard gallop, Escobar anxious to overtake them.

Suddenly, Escobar's prey reined up and dismounted.

The three men tossed their revolvers to the ground, then raised their hands high above their heads and waited, trusting that their act of surrender would spare their lives. As we pulled to a sliding stop and surrounded the trio, their thin, tired horses drifted slowly away to graze on a tiny patch of yellowed grass.

With guns drawn, we stared at the pitiful figures. Their pantalones and camisas were torn and filthy, looking like old clothes robbed from the corpses of men long dead. One had no boots and stood barefoot on the stony ground. Their dirty hair lay flat and matted under ragged straw sombreros. Each man had dried blood on his cotton camisa. Two of them had deep scratches on their faces, raw places not yet scabbed over.

The only sound I could hear was that of my horse blowing. My heart thudded so hard in my chest that I grasped the saddle horn to still my shaking. I knew these men did not have long to live.

Escobar dismounted, the creaking of his saddle loud in the llano silence. With a heavy Colt .45 in hand and hatred in his dust-reddened eyes, he approached the three men who backed away until they came up against our horses. Chávez placed the tip of his rifle against the spine of one and pushed him back toward Escobar. No one spoke. A gust of wind skittered silica grains across the floor of the plain.

Pointing his revolver at the closest man, Escobar asked, "What is your name?"

Trembling, he replied, "Salazar."

When addressed in a like manner the others yielded the names Mondragón and Téllez. Turning back to Salazar, the only one whose face was not scratched, Escobar raised his revolver and laid the end of the barrel against the man's chest. He then looked up at

Borrego and me, seated on our horses directly behind Salazar, and motioned for us to move away.

He lowered his gaze and looked into the eyes of Salazar, stating calmly, "She was my daughter."

The expressions on the faces of the three men covered over with a deep sheen of terror, and they shook uncontrollably. They had the look of men who knew they were about to die.

Mondragón whined, "Please, please, please."

A wet stain spread across the front of his pantalones. Téllez reached out both hands in a pleading gesture, tears in his eyes, then held on to Mondragón to keep from collapsing.

Escobar, still holding the revolver to Salazar's heart, asked, "Which one of you killed my daughter?"

The men pointed at one another, gibbering accusations and blame. Escobar smiled. We sat grim-faced in our saddles.

"*¡Silencio!*" Escobar barked, and they fell quiet.

Mondragón dropped to his knees and whimpered like a dog, but Escobar ordered him to stand.

My gray, sensing the tension and fear, tossed his head nervously. Pointing toward the two men with scratches on their faces, Escobar commanded us to shoot them in the legs if they tried to run.

Turning back to Salazar, he lowered his revolver, pulled the trigger, and disintegrated the vaquero's right foot. Salazar dropped to the ground. His scream, puncturing the llano air like a razored dagger, startled my horse into a series of quicksteps and caused the flesh on my forearms to prickle.

Black blood poured from the open wound onto the sand and gravel of the desert floor, soaking into the parched soil. Eyes running over with tears, Mondragón and Téllez stuttered prayers to whatever god they held dear.

Escobar summoned Borrego and me to dismount and hold the flopping Salazar still. I did not want to touch the fallen man with my hands, so I placed a booted foot on one of his arms. Borrego did the same with the left leg. Escobar straddled the shocked victim and glared until Salazar finally met his gaze.

"Are you in pain?" he asked.

"*Sí, Sí, Sí,*" Salazar blubbered, and in the next breath begged for mercy.

"I will give you mercy," Escobar said, "when I am finished with you."

With that, he stepped a pace backward and fired another round into Salazar's right knee, the large-caliber bullet separating the lower leg from the thigh. Bits of shattered white bone in a matrix of flesh and blood were carried along in the stream that gushed from the wound, thickened, then ceased movement. Salazar's cotton pantalones smoldered as a result of the proximity of the blast.

Escobar never stopped smiling.

"Did you show my daughter any mercy?" he asked.

The left knee was next, and the bullet, slamming into the recumbent man, came within two inches of Borrego's boot. A stream of blood flowed out from beneath Salazar's leg as he keened guttural moans. Though he no longer moved, Borrego and I still kept our weight on him.

Mondragón started to run, but the simultaneous cocking of three revolvers stayed him. He looked into the faces of El Enano, Sánchez, and Chávez, hoping to find some ray of salvation, some sign of surviving the nightmare. He found none.

I watched dry-mouthed as Escobar holstered his revolver and withdrew a long knife from his sash. The handle was made from human bone, and the oft-nicked blade, honed sharp, hissed as it moved through the dry air.

Bending low, Escobar sawed through the cotton rope that served as a belt to Salazar's pantalones, then cut away the cloth to expose a gaunt abdomen, pale as the underbelly of a snake. Deftly, Escobar sliced into the flesh, cutting only the tissue, nothing more, making a clean incision across the belly from hip to hip. Borrego and I watched as a fist-sized knot of pink gut pushed through the opening, followed by a fetid odor that caused my throat to constrict. Reaching down, Escobar grabbed the slippery intestine, pulled most of its length out of the cavity, and dropped it onto the sand. Sánchez stepped away, stumbled beyond the ring of horses, and vomited.

Escobar sheathed his knife and dragged a length of the warm gut up to the dying man's head and held it before his bulging eyes. Fine particles of sand coated the intestine where it had flopped onto the ground. Hundreds of flies attracted by the smell swarmed and landed. Red ants crawled up its length.

Moving as if he had done it a hundred times, Escobar wrapped the *tripa* around Salazar's neck, and with slow and deliberate movements, strangled him, enjoying every second. Finished, he stepped back, wiped his bloody hands on the dead man's camisa, and admired his work.

When I was certain Salazar was dead, I removed my booted foot from his arm and went to stand beside the gray, my knees shaking as I held on to the saddle for support.

• • •

For the next two hours Escobar tortured Mondragón and Téllez, their screams filling the llano, displacing the wind, bouncing back to us over and over from the distant ridges. Without uttering so much as a single word, Chávez, Borrego, Sánchez, El Enano, and I watched. Borrego finally placed his hands over his ears. Sánchez turned away and cried. El Enano focused his eyes on his horse's mane and prayed.

The expression on Chávez's face never changed.

I watched Escobar. He never stopped smiling as he skinned, disemboweled, and then dismembered Mondragón and Téllez, keeping them alive as long as he could.

"*Madre de Dios,*" I whispered to no one in particular. "Why am I here?"

• • •

As a crimson sun sank beneath the western ridge, the pieces of the three dead men's bodies were tossed into the single shallow grave we had dug. We smoothed them over, but no markers were erected. All that remained were bloodstained sand and rock.

Within days, I knew that the llano wind would erase any sign of what happened here, but nothing, neither rain nor wind nor time, would erase it from my mind, my dreams.

The Priest

El Sacerdote

The destruction of San Benito was complete: cornfields set afire, livestock slaughtered, homes burned and razed. Of the forty or so residents, fifteen men, women, and children were dead. The rest had been driven away, carrying their injured with them.

Bodies were piled on the steps of the church. Two of the men had been beheaded, two more scalped, their bloody, hairless skulls abuzz with flies. Three bodies were sprawled on the ground in the tiny plaza in front of the church, the afternoon shadow of the roof-mounted crucifix patterned across one of them, a girl, nude. Two dogs sniffed the corpses. An old woman, about sixty years or so, had been stripped, flayed, raped, and her skull crushed. Two girls, both dead, had their breasts sliced away. Behind the church, three babies were impaled on fence posts.

San Benito was no more.

When we arrived, Chávez, Sánchez, and Borrego studied the tracks. We followed the sign and found the survivors at a poor camp set up about a half mile away near a bend in the river. Frightened, convinced we were the raiders returned to kill more of them, they hid among the trees.

Recognizing Chávez, one of the old men stepped from his hiding place, hobbled up to him on a cane, and said, "There were twenty of them, all mounted, all armed. The workers, the men toiling in the corn, could not defend themselves. They were shot in the back as they fled."

"The women were herded into the church," the old man said. "The young girl there was to be married next week. She was attacked by the riders who pulled her clothes away. She fought back only to have her throat slit. Two of them raped her as she bled to death on the floor next to the altar. They carried her out of the church and threw her onto the ground."

"*¿El sacerdote?*" Chávez asked.

"The priest offered no resistance," replied the old man. "He only stood and watched. He has not even come out here to see to our welfare."

"Mueller's vaqueros?"

"*Sí*," the old man affirmed. He hesitated a moment, then added, "*El sacerdote* dined with Señor Joaquín Mueller at his rancho only a week ago."

Chávez stiffened. "Where is *el sacerdote*?"

The old man shrugged and said, "*¿Quién sabe?* Probably still in the church. He was not harmed."

Chávez called for Borrego, El Enano, and me to follow him, and we rode back through the village to the church. Embers from the burned-out casas still smoldered, thin plumes of smoke curling skyward.

Dismounting, Chávez pulled his maguey from the leather thong where it hung on the saddle. Leaving Pesadilla ground-hitched, he signaled for us to remain where we were, then strode through the double wooden doors, rope in hand.

Minutes later, Chávez reappeared leading the neck-roped priest down the stone steps to where we sat our mounts. The priest clutched a bulging canvas bag to his breast. Turning to Borrego, Chávez ordered him to summon all of the villagers to the church. A half hour passed and the survivors of San Benito arrived and stood in a tight circle around Chávez and the sacerdote.

Chávez addressed la gente. "The priest has admitted that he accepted a large amount of money from hacendado Mueller. It seems he was given the money in exchange for information on the comings and goings of your men and on the number and kinds of guns in your village."

"No, no," the priest whimpered. "No! It is not true." Sweat poured from his brow and upper lip.

He looked around at the assembled campesinos and said, "The money was only intended for the church, for the betterment of our pueblo."

The priest's gaze faltered from the hardened stares of la gente, his shoulders slumped.

Chávez moved to within inches of the priest's sweating face. Fixing the holy man's eyes with his own, he asked, "Tell me, Father, what do you know of hell?"

The priest tried to effect a regal bearing but stammered, "I, I don't know what you mean."

Chávez smiled thinly and said, "You are about to learn."

He snatched the bag from the priest's grasp, opened it, and dumped the contents onto the ground. Coins clinked to the dusty street, paper bills fluttered to the ground.

"No!" cried the priest as he stooped to retrieve the money. "It is for the church!"

A light gust of wind scattered the bills among the legs of the onlookers. Chávez said, "Pick up the money and divide it among you."

Turning to El Enano, he gestured toward the church and said, "Take anything made of gold or silver, give it to the village blacksmith to melt down, then divide it among them also."

Grabbing at Chávez's camisa with bony hands, the priest sobbed, "Leave the church alone! It is sacred! You, of all people, cannot violate it!"

Chávez slapped away the Jesuit's hands.

"You have already violated it, you *cabrón*. As for me, nothing is sacred any longer."

Stabbing a finger into the priest's chest, Chávez said, "You are a liar. You are a thief. You are as much a murderer as if you had fired the guns yourself. You are to blame for these rapes and killings as much as hacendado Mueller and his *pinche* vaqueros. I cannot decide whether to hang you or simply shoot you."

The old man who spoke with Chávez earlier stepped out of the crowd and said, "*Por favor*, Señor Chávez. Give him to us."

Chávez studied the old man, then la gente, then the priest. Finally, he handed the end of the rope to the old man. Wordlessly, the elder tugged the rope sharply and led the holy man away. The crowd parted to allow passage, and then closed in behind and followed.

Still mounted, Chávez addressed us. "Tonight we feed and rest. Tomorrow, we ride to Mueller's rancho."

That evening in camp, I sat next to Chávez as we dined on corn, frijoles, and tortillas. When he finished eating, I asked him to tell me about hacendado Mueller.

Staring into the clear, starlit night sky, Chávez remained motionless and silent for several minutes. After taking a deep breath, he turned to me, his black eyes reflecting the starlight.

"Joaquín Mueller's father arrived here before the time the Great War was fought across the ocean," he said. "The old man coveted the fertile and productive lands of the *indios,* the campesinos. Mueller took a Mexican wife, made friends with many *politicos* in Mexico City, and with the help of lawyers and *federales*, moved onto our homelands, displacing *la gente*. When we refused to leave, Mueller had us beaten, killed."

Chávez looked away, deep into the nearby canyon, gathering his thoughts and, I imagined, trying to keep a rein on his emotions. Presently, his attention returned.

"Mueller drove many of us out and stocked our lands with his cattle. When we fought back, he turned his rank of vaqueros into a small army, armed them, and set them loose on the countryside. The old man is dead now some ten years, but his son, Joaquín, is worse, more ambitious, reckless, vicious."

I absorbed all of what Chávez said. I thought of what El Enano told me about the senseless massacre of his family. I thought about the good people of San Benito.

I was so deep in my thoughts that I startled when Chávez spoke again.

"I will have no rest until Joaquín Mueller is dead."

I looked up to respond, but Chávez was gone.

• • •

One hour past dawn we rode out of the campsite with our canteens filled, our saddlebags packed with tortillas and dried *carne*, our weapons cleaned and loaded. We faced a two-day ride, but we were eager to revenge the depredations of San Benito.

When we guided our caballos through the devastated pueblo, we came upon the priest. From the *vigas* of a burned-out home, the men of the pueblo had fashioned a ten-foot-high cross, which they had planted directly in front of the church. Upon the cross hung the priest, naked but for a vicious headpiece of mesquite thorns. Blood streamed from his bald pate down his face and into his eyes and ears, down his neck and onto his torso. His upper arms were lashed to the crosspiece. Heavy railroad spikes had been hammered through each palm. Another spike impaled both feet, which had been crudely broken. The fresh blood, dripping onto the sandy ground, had drawn dogs, swine, and flies. Twin crows perched on the crossbeam.

We reined up. El Enano turned away, his expression suggesting he did not believe this sacrilege worthy of warriors.

Sánchez made the sign of the cross and muttered, "*¡Dios mio!*" He saw us watching, and he looked down, embarrassed.

Chávez could not restrain a slight smile.

A dark sense of foreboding closed around me, a frightening feeling that this mad act would soon open the gates of Hades for all of us. Though the morning was warm, I shivered.

A hissing release of air issued from the priest's parched, cracked lips. We moved our horses closer so we could make out his slurred words.

"Kill me," he breathed.

Chávez pulled his revolver and aimed it at the heart of the sacerdote. We waited.

Ten seconds passed before he lowered the weapon and reseated it in his holster. Looking up at the priest, he said, "You have not suffered enough. Ask me again when I return in three days."

He whirled Pesadilla and kicked him into a trot up the road toward the west. We followed.

The Last Ride

El Paseo Último

While the others made certain no one was about, I cut the fences somewhere along the eastern boundary of hacendado Mueller's extensive rancho. Within minutes, Sánchez, Olguín, and Jaramillo herded seventeen head of prime cattle through the opening. Chávez instructed them to deliver the stock to the survivors at San Benito. Chávez led the rest of us—El Enano, Borrego, Herrera, and myself—across the pasture in search of the ranch headquarters, in search of the men who had destroyed San Benito.

We did not know what would happen on arriving at the Mueller rancho, and we did not ask. Silenced by the hard, determined look in Chávez's eyes, we only knew that some would die.

Last in a single file of riders as we traversed the pasture, I peered through the twilight settling across the fields and shadowing the adjacent woods. I fought off a sinister feeling about the night that had drawn close around us. I watched the men ahead of me and wondered who would live, who would die.

• • •

Illuminated only by a rising quarter-moon and a few stars, we tied our caballos to some stunted bushes in a dry wash and climbed to a low rise. Lying flat on our bellies, we looked down into a wide valley. The main ranch house and grounds where Mueller resided, all enclosed by an eight-foot-tall adobe wall, lay a mile or more in the distance.

• • •

Near the bottom of the sloping ridge from which we observed, light from gas lanterns filtered out of the curtained windows of the vaqueros' quarters—small cabins, twelve in all.

To the south of the cabins were a large barn, a blacksmith shop, and corrals. Forty or fifty horses grazed in a fenced meadow beyond. Two dozen men and women went about their evening chores. Indiscernible bits of conversation carried on the night air. We heard laughter, occasionally a curse. Above us, clouds came together in a dark roil.

"They are many," Borrego said. "We are only five."

Chávez silenced him with a stare. He looked back at the cluster of cabins and the people, then said, "Four of us will approach on foot, one will remain with the *caballos*."

We looked at each other. Who would be told to stay? Who would be given the job of a boy? Who would not be permitted to join in the fight? I guessed El Enano would be selected to watch the mounts.

Looking at me, Chávez said, "Carlos, it is your responsibility."

I said nothing, but inside I cursed the embarrassing assignment. I, a fighter, a warrior taught by Chávez himself, was to remain with the horses. El Enano, sensing my disappointment, gripped my arm and said, "It is best that you remain. It is more important than you think."

Making certain none of the others could hear, he lowered his voice and said, "It is good that you do not go with us this night."

Pointing to the large herd of caballos beyond the corrals, Chávez said, "Borrego, Herrera, you will go with me to cut the fences and herd the horses back to the wash where ours are tied."

"El Enano, you will crawl down the slope to the barn and set it afire."

The dwarf nodded.

Chávez continued. "It will serve as a distraction while the horses are moved. We will reunite back at this ridge. When they come for us, for the horses, afoot, we will kill them all."

• • •

We waited in silence until just before midnight. After checking the loads in our revolvers once again, Chávez pulled the sombrero from El Enano's knobby head and rubbed his skull. He was followed by Herrera and Borrego.

When my turn came, the dwarf embraced me and wished me luck. Pulling me down close to his face, he whispered, "I will not be returning. I know this to be true. *Vaya con Dios, hermano*."

Before I could reply, El Enano abruptly turned and shuffled away, dropped to his hands and knees, and alternately crawled and slid down the grassy slope toward the barn, keeping low to the ground.

Slamming with urgent impact, the dark feeling that had come to me earlier in the day returned. I wanted to grab Chávez and tell him something was wrong, that this was not to be our night, but he was gone, working his way down the slope with Borrego and Herrera.

I wanted to call out to them, to stop them, but they were now too far away. I was left alone with the caballos.

Ten minutes later, in dim moonlight, I watched the silhouetted figures of Chávez, Borrego, and Herrera cut the pasture fence and pull the wires back to provide an opening for the horses.

I saw El Enano enter the barn.

As Chávez, Herrera, and Borrego moved smoke-quiet among the herd of horses, a sudden shout echoed out of the barn, followed by three gunshots. Lights flared up in the cabins and half-dressed vaqueros carrying revolvers and rifles streamed out of the doors, casting about for the source of the disturbance.

A moment later, a burly vaquero strode out of the barn carrying the hatless dwarf under one arm. He threw El Enano to the ground and kicked him hard, again and again. The dwarf tried to rise and I could see he had been shot and was badly wounded. The vaquero kicked him twice more and then held him down with a heavy, booted foot.

A circle of men and women quickly ringed the pair. Sounds of anger and confusion among the residents of the tiny community surged up the ridge to where I lay. One of the women made the sign of the cross.

Someone barked a command and a few moments later a saddled and bridled horse was ridden from the nearby corral. The rider shook out a reata and cast a loop over the dwarf's head. With a yell, he spurred the caballo into a gallop. As the rope twanged taut, El Enano was jerked from his place on the ground and dragged, bouncing along the stony road behind the horse.

The rider made two long passes in front of the barn and cabins, finally sliding his mount to a stop in front of the gathered onlookers. Even through the darkness I could see El Enano lying skinned and bloodied on the ground. Feebly, he reached up and out with a diminutive arm. Mercilessly, the crowd fell upon him, fists and feet inflicting uncommon damage.

The rider shouted again, quirted his horse, and sped away, El Enano's body flopping along behind like a cloth doll. Back and forth, over and over again, the horseman dragged the dwarf across the rough ground. I gritted my teeth as tears streamed down my face and soaked the ground beneath me.

Another shout alerted the onlookers to the escaping horses and the three dark figures rushing up the grassy slope. Several vaqueros set off afoot in pursuit; others went to saddle horses in the corral, horses we had not seen earlier.

Chávez, Herrera, and Borrego arrived breathless. Pausing only long enough to grab a handful of my shirt and jerk me to my feet, Chávez said, "There are too many of them. We must ride."

With clenched jaw, I knocked his hand away and said, "El Enano is dead."

Chávez stiffened at this news and was about to say something when the clamor of the pursuers riding and running up the slope alerted us to the danger of our predicament.

We ran to the horses, untied them, and mounted. I led El Enano's pony by the reins as the four of us goaded our mounts into a gallop toward the break we had made in the east fence. Seventy-five yards behind us, riders surged over the rise, yelling, cursing, firing their weapons.

Their horses, well rested and excited by the chase, gained on us, bullets singing closer and closer. My gray stumbled and I felt us going down, but I yanked on the reins and he recovered and regained his balance, and we pushed forward.

As we rode through the break in the fence, Chávez instructed us to split up. Without stopping, Borrego and Herrera spurred south and sped along the road.

With the pursuers only seconds away, Chávez reined up next to me, placed a hand on my arm, and said, "We will get them another time." He wheeled Pesadilla and plunged into the wooded bottomlands to the east.

Still leading El Enano's horse, I reined north and fled back toward San Benito.

Blood

El Sangre

Two days following the encounter at the Mueller rancho, my caballo carried me into the plaza of what was left of the village of San Benito.

The priest still hung from the crude cross. His eyes, plucked out by crows, were gone, and maggots wriggled in the streaming sockets. Swarms of flies covered the wounds on his hands and feet. At the base of the cross, the sand was a dark crimson-brown. In the middle of the dried blood a sow slept in the sun.

I cursed, spat at the circle of dried blood, and rode through the village.

Some small amount of work rebuilding the pueblo had taken place during our absence, but with few exceptions most of la gente still lived in the temporary camp near the stream.

When they saw me riding toward the little settlement, they ran out and greeted me, embracing me when I stepped down from my horse. As we spoke, their dark eyes searched behind me for the rest of the band.

The Resurrection

La Resurrección

For three weeks I remained with the survivors of San Benito, helping them construct temporary shelters, helping them replant their corn and calabazas, helping them bury their dead.

I raked the ashes and cinders from their former homes. I cut, peeled, and shaped juniper logs to be used in the building of new casas and the rebuilding of the old. I harvested cane from the river bottoms to be used for roofs and fences. I worked side by side with a boy who spoke softly of his hope that they could live in peace, without fear of raids from Mueller's vaqueros. He said he wished for a wife and children to raise, sons and daughters who would help him hoe the corn and harvest the squash and share the bounty. I gave him El Enano's pony because he didn't have one.

I watched as what was left of the tiny community gathered to participate in the funerals for the dead who had lain in state for several days as la gente prayed over the bodies. Neighbors, friends, relatives dug the graves, constructed the caskets, carried out the ceremonies, joined together to cook and eat and talk of beginning anew. I worked alongside them.

There were celebrations. The funerals, ongoing acts of love, were followed by gatherings where everyone set aside their grief, where everyone danced and sang and enjoyed the notion that the departed ones were now exempt from the cares, worries, and hardships of this life. La gente invited me to participate in the ceremonies and I did.

At night around the campfires I listened as they talked about death as if it were an old friend, one they were well prepared to host. Death, to them, a mere moment in the infinite web of time, was accepted and even embraced. I listened as they talked about their hopes of rebuilding their homes, their village. Never once did they mention the church.

Some of la gente asked about the raid, about what happened at the Mueller ranch. I could not speak of it. El Enano, the pathetic, bent, warted creature who possessed a heart full of love and to whom life had not been kind, El Enano my friend, was gone, and the grief was almost too much for me to bear. After a while the villagers no longer asked. They honored my silence as I honored theirs.

When I could not sleep, I walked alone along the stream that flowed past the north end of the village and cried copious tears. I cried for El Enano. I cried for myself.

Sitting beneath a roble in the dark, sometimes I thought I could hear the music from El Enano's fiddle. I imagined it to be so and many nights I fell asleep to the lullabies.

One evening as a strong wind whistled through the trees, I thought I heard a familiar voice coming from the north, the border. The voice was that of El Enano, and it was crying: *vaya cuando puedes, vaya cunado puedes.*

When much of the work of rebuilding was done, most of the casas finished, I grew anxious and restless. I wanted to go away, wished to be on the move though I knew not where. To seek my compañeros? To ride once more with Chávez? The thread that had connected us had been broken and it left me wondering. Would it ever be the same?

Something vital had been wrung from me, something permanently lost that I could never regain, but I didn't know what else to do. I packed my few belongings, saddled the gray, and rode southward to find Chávez.

The Peace

La Paz

As my caballo grazed close by, as a stolen chicken sizzled on the spit above the fire, I washed trail dust from my hands, arms, and face.

Fed by a singing spring that bled from a nearby limestone outcrop, the clear pool of cold, blue water was balm for my injured and aching body, a salve for my troubled heart. I removed my clothes and dropped naked to the fine sandy bottom, allowing the chill water to cool, to soothe, to regenerate.

Once, staring at the surface of the pool, I saw my reflection in the water. The image was of a man I did not recognize. My face, deeply tanned and almost as dark as Herrera's, sported an untrimmed moustache and a scraggly beard. My hair hung to my shoulders. With a hand, I felt the beard, the flesh. It felt as though I was touching someone else.

The eyes gave me a start and held my attention. The eyes were set deeper in my skull than I remembered, darker than I recalled. The eyes appeared as hard as black agate marbles and belonged to someone I did not know.

Following a meal of roasted chicken with wild garlic, wild onions, wild grapes, and a few peaches stolen from a church orchard I had passed earlier in the day, I laid back, using my blood-speckled saddle for a pillow. The thick, lush grass upon which I reclined offered more comfort than I had felt in weeks.

It was the only peace I had known since crossing the Río Grande last spring and entering this land of poverty and passion, of repression and conflict, of celebration and mourning, of mystery and magic.

Of death and rebirth.

The Spirit

El Espíritu

The campesinos and the indios said that he came like the wind, moved like the wind. Some said he was the wind. They said that he appeared to those who dared to tread the forbidden land of the Apache, the Yaqui, the Tarahumara, the Otomi, in the remote confines and barrancas of the Sierra Madre Occidental.

Wraithlike, smokelike, he hovered above the dying coals of my campfire, holding aloft in his left hand a bloody bundle of dark hair, the scalp of someone who sought to remove him from his chosen land. Crimson droplets, pip-pip-pipping, fell from the scalp and struck the heated stones encircling the low fire, making a faint hiss that fingered through the intervening air.

• • •

Morning.

Waking from the strange dream, I threw back my thin serape and rose from the rocky ground to kneel before the ringed ashes and tried to coax a flame from the fading embers.

Then I saw them. A dozen or more sanguine spots of scabbed blood patterned along three of the stones.

I stood and turned to see if he was still there, if he had come for me.

I was alone.

I knelt once more to tend the fire. My caballo, hobbled in the young grass several yards away, jerked his head, and I followed the direction to which his attentive ears pointed. Materializing out of the rock like a mirage, the poncho-cloaked Indian stood by the stone outcrop, the crucifix-shaped scar on his face bone-white in the early sun, his bare feet buried in the fine mist that swirled up from the pool.

His eyes clamped onto mine, and he said, "Will you ride once more with Chávez?"

The Tarantulas

Las Tarántulas

Tomasito reached across the embers of the campfire to fill my cup from the battered and fire-blackened coffeepot. Nodding my gratitude, I savored the dark brew, made the way the campesinos preferred it—laced with sugar and goat milk. I sipped quietly as I watched the other new riders—Martínez, Garza, and Hidalgo—arrange their blankets for sleep.

Chávez, who seldom slept in camp, had ridden away into a nearby canyon. El Enano once told me that the leader went away by himself to speak with the sprits of the family he had lost.

Tomasito was the youngest, the most inexperienced of the new riders, but he was eager to learn, to contribute. He wanted so badly to be a fighter, to accompany us across the mountains and plains. Yet he seemed so fragile, so vulnerable, when he had kissed his mother good-bye. As we sat our horses and waited, his old, plump mother was reluctant to release Tomasito from her embrace. When she finally did, she made him accept a basket of tortillas, bread, corn, cabrito, and pork. When he broke away and mounted, tears spilled from her eyes, sorrow clinging to her like a fine mist. I turned back as we rode away and saw her in the shaded doorway of the jacal, wringing the hem of her apron, fussing at her hair, crying at the departure of her only son. Though he tried to hide them, I also saw tears in Tomasito's eyes.

Skilled and gentle with the horses, Tomasito had been asked to break and train the new ones for our band. His manner was not brutal like Olguín and others. Instead, he spoke softly to the animals, spent hours working with them, talking and singing to them. He treated them with kindness.

Tomasito could shoot a pistola well, but he had never killed a man. One day, as he watched a death at my hands, I realized he never could. I knew Tomasito was unsure of himself, hesitant, frightened. I knew he did not share our mission, the rightness of our goal.

One night, we learned of Tomasito's great fear. Reynaldo Garza, reclining next to me by the campfire, called the young wrangler's attention to a large tarantula crawling slowly across his booted foot. Eyes wide, Tomasito screamed, a spine-racking, terror-filled shriek. He leaped to his feet and, with a series of barely controlled jerks and starts, kicked the bristled creature into the embers.

Trying desperately not to shake, Tomasito reseated himself and pulled his serape tight around his shoulders. Olguín stared at the sizzling spider, its burning limbs curling into a tight, eight-legged fist, and said, "It is the season for them to migrate. There will be more. Many more."

For the rest of the night, Tomasito huddled in his blanket beside the fire, shaking and peering into the darkness, watching for more spiders. I know he claimed no sleep that night.

Midmorning of the next day found us following a trail that paralleled a deep arroyo on our way to Madera. Hidalgo, riding near the head of the file behind Chávez, pulled his mount to a stop and pointed into the narrow, forty-foot-deep, sandy chasm. At the bottom, thousands of the giant spiders moved in a series of black waves, a mass of writhing, hairy bodies that stretched from one side of the wide arroyo to the other. A carpet of arachnids, they generated a faint hiss as they crawled over one another, abrading bristles, and making their way to some unknown destination.

Paralyzed, Tomasito stared. His skittish colt, sensing his fear, danced nervous, uncertain steps close to the edge of the arroyo, yet Tomasito, transfixed, made no attempt to control the animal.

The right rear foot of the horse broke through the loose soil of the rim, threatening its balance. For one incredible second, horse and rider remained motionless in midair, perched above the abyss, almost angelic in attitude. Then they disappeared over the edge, plummeting, screaming, to the bottom.

The colt, with flailing broken legs, tried to rise. Tomasito, thrown clear, landed in the middle of the swarm of spiders. At first his frenzied arms moved frantically as he brushed the tarantulas from his face and body, his screams piercing our souls. Moments later, weaker, he moved more slowly, then ceased movement and sound altogether as hundreds of the spiders covered him and his dying horse.

Shaken, Olguín said, "It will be two days and two nights before they pass through."

Chávez peered into the arroyo at the screaming horse. Pulling his rifle from the side-mounted scabbard, he cocked it, took careful aim, and fired. The horse lay still. Chávez moved the weapon slightly to take aim at the unmoving spider-covered form that was Tomasito, held the point for a few seconds, then lowered the gun.

Chávez's brooding eyes regarded each of us as he said, "There is nothing more we can do. We must ride."

• • •

That night, while the others slept, I sat in the flickering light of the low campfire thinking about young Tomasito. I poured my own coffee from the blackened, crinkled pot.

I watched as a lone tarantula crawled across the toe of my boot.

The Screams

Los Chillidos

Next to El Enano, Rafael Herrera had been my closest friend among the riders, *mi amigo, mi hermano*. We had shared food, bullets, horses. He had even offered to share his women with me, but I was shy, ignorant, and felt clumsy because I had never been with a woman before.

Herrera and I had shared the blood surge of victories and the blood loss of defeat. Herrera loved to kill and believed he only executed men who deserved killing.

"For some," said Herrera, "killing is a skill, one that can be refined, appreciated, even admired."

For Herrera, he admitted easily, it was also a need.

"It is nothing to kill," he said, "but for some men, men who have no stomach for such things, it is sometimes hard to live with."

Herrera was convinced he was performing a valuable service by killing as many of the vaqueros as he did. He took pride in his ability to slay a man and think nothing of it.

Herrera never manifested any remorse for killing men. While he claimed the men he killed deserved it, the truth was that he took pleasure in taking lives. Killing was like a drug for him—if Herrera went more than three or four days without killing someone, he grew edgy, irritable.

Herrera had saved my life more than once when we fought together, and we had fought side by side too many times to count. I wanted to know what had happened to him, what made him the killer of men, and why, for him, it was so easy and for others so difficult, but I could not bring myself to ask.

• • •

Herrera arrived in camp one afternoon wearing knee-high, pliable leather riding boots that he ordered from Europe. On them he had fastened heavy, silver Mexican spurs that jingled loudly when he walked. He strutted like a cock, displaying his boots for us. We applauded, and Sánchez and Borrego offered hearty, admiring whistles. Hearing the sound of his own spurs along with the shouts of approval from his compañeros, Herrera smiled broadly.

Two long-barreled revolvers hung from his belt and a single-shot derringer resided in his sash. Twin fighting knives were sheathed to each holster, the scabbards added by a boot-maker in Ciudad Chihuahua. Herrera employed his knives to slit throats, pluck out eyeballs, and slice the hamstrings of prisoners when they refused to talk. These knives were used to elicit painful screams from those who would not do his bidding.

Full bandoleras crisscrossed Herrera's chest, the shining bullets newly polished. Herrera prided himself in always looking good, always being prepared to kill.

When he spotted me, he strode over and we embraced. I grinned, happy and relieved at his return.

Around his waist he had buckled a money belt crammed full with gold and silver coins, most of them, I was certain, taken from the pockets of men he had slain in battle.

Around his neck, plain to see, Herrera wore a gold crucifix, dangling from a gold chain.

• • •

Two weeks later, high in the Sierra Madres, we came to a stream swollen deep and wide with recent early autumn rains. Chávez sat Pesadilla quietly for several minutes near the flooded bank and contemplated the surging river.

"We should wait to cross," he said. "It will be one day, perhaps two at the most, before the water recedes enough."

Laughing, displaying his roosterlike bravado, Herrera called us old women, saying it was only water. He spurred his gelding into the raging stream. As the water swirled around the caballo's flanks,

Herrera provided a joyous shout and said, "I will show you how it is done!"

The swift current took the gelding's legs out from under him and the frightened animal went down, emitting a terror-driven scream that froze the marrow of my bones. A second later, Herrera, sinking from the weight of his boots, spurs, revolvers, bandoleras, and coin-filled money pouch, was swept away and under, his own screams intermingling with those of his gelding, screams that hung in the air long after he disappeared.

Chávez shifted his weight in the saddle and with no emotion whatsoever stated, "This river, the Río Bavispe, will carry him to the Río Yaqui, which flows into the great sea that lies between mainland Sonora and the Baja peninsula, a place he always wanted to visit. At least he died wealthy."

• • •

Not far from the flooded bank, we warmed ourselves around a fire as Chávez, with uncharacteristic garrulousness, talked about Herrera's uncle.

"His name was Rodolfo Fierro," he said, "and he was a close friend and trusted officer of Pancho Villa. Villa made Fierro a colonel in his army."

"Like Herrera, Fierro was a killer," sad Chávez, "a man born to the profession, a man who found intense satisfaction, pleasure, and even comfort in taking the life of another."

Chávez paused long enough to sip hot coffee from his cup. "Fierro once told Villa that he suffered indigestion if he was unable to kill at least one man before breakfast.

"Once, when Villa's forces stopped a train, about a dozen gringos, all on the payroll of the Mexican government, were forced out of their passenger car and made to stand in a line. Fierro calmly stepped from one to the other, shooting each in the head until all had been killed. It was said he laughed as he fired his revolvers.

"On another occasion, Fierro emptied out a federal prison, instructing the inmates to gather in the yard. While one of his lieutenants reloaded his revolvers, Fierro shot all ninety-nine of them, stopping only long enough to enjoy a cup of coffee and exchange jokes with men who were to die at his hand only minutes later."

Chávez took another sip and said, "It is strange. Fierro died in exactly the same manner as our amigo, our brother Herrera, pulled under the waters of a rain-swollen stream by the weight of his weapons, gear, and money."

While the others organized camp, I sat in stunned silence and watched the thick, muddy water rush past.

• • •

That night, when I finally slept, I dreamed I was in a small skiff on the Gulf of California. As I rowed the boat to some destination unclear, I thought I saw something in the distance out on the water, an object floating alone. I blinked hard and it was gone. I blinked again and it was back. I rose up in the boat, shielded the sun from my eyes, and peered into the distance for a better look. Suddenly, I heard screams arriving with the waves on the water.

Herrera's screams.

Or the screams of Herrera's ghost.

• • •

All night, the sound of the rushing stream argued with Herrera's screams that rose up from somewhere inside of me, bursting out, echoing off the rock walls, but heard by no one but me.

The screams never stopped.

The Voice

La Voz

A palpable aura of gloom pervaded the camp for days. Chávez came and went with no obvious purpose. The recent losses of El Enano, Tomasito, and Herrera weighed heavily on every member of the band, and it felt as though a significant amount of our spirit had been sucked away. Four straight days of rain did little to dispel the gloom. The thick, dark clouds scudded low and heavy over the mountains and canyons, dropping their loads of moisture.

"This time of year," said Borrego, "the rain could go on for days without stopping."

• • •

Bad luck did not cease with Herrera's death. Olguín sliced away the tip of the trigger finger on his right hand while dressing a deer. Without treating the wound, he continued with the butchering, then rode into a nearby canyon with Jaramillo to hunt for quail. The next day, the finger was so badly infected that Olguín was unable to use his hand. When Chávez returned to lead us on a scouting expedition, he ordered Olguín to remain in camp, telling him he would be useless if we encountered Mueller's vaqueros and were forced to fight.

Following a week of herbal infusions, the infection left, but Olguín never regained complete use of his hand. He was never able to pull the trigger on a revolver again. A valuable and skilled fighter, Olguín, like El Enano and Herrera, was now lost to us, reduced to fetching wood and performing camp chores.

One of the new riders, Hidalgo, was struck in the right forearm by a large cascabel while gathering firewood. Jaramillo tried to dress the wound with moss and spider web, but Hidalgo refused, insisting it was nothing and continuing with his chores. An hour later, he grew nauseous, had seizures, and fainted. Sánchez and I dragged him to the shade where Jaramillo cared for him.

In the full moonlight of that night, I could see Hidalgo's forearm was swollen to twice its normal size, the skin stretched so tightly that I thought it would split. The entire arm was purple. Hidalgo now had a raging fever that Jaramillo tried to control with bandannas soaked in water from the nearby stream. All the while he sat by Hidalgo treating his arm and his fever, Jaramillo wished for El Enano.

Hidalgo survived the snakebite but only regained partial use of his arm. When he was able to ride, Chávez sent him home.

• • •

One afternoon Sánchez rode into camp with the body of another new rider, Garza, tied to the back of his caballo. Garza had been out hunting and was apparently surprised by a contingent of Mueller's vaqueros. When Sánchez found his body, it was stripped of weapons, bandoleras, and boots, and his caballo was missing. Jaramillo counted eighteen bullet holes in the body. Garza's cojones had been sliced off and stuffed into his mouth.

• • •

For days the clouds hovered over the canyon where we were camped, adding to the despair. Mechanically, I busied myself with chores and tending the remuda, but my foreboding grew. It was an intense feeling, similar to the one I harbored weeks earlier as I rode with Chávez, El Enano, and the others onto the rancho of hacendado Mueller.

The shift in fortune concerned me, caused me to wonder what else could go wrong, to wonder who might be next to die. The clouds, darker and lower, threatened to descend to the camp and cover us all. The last new rider, Martínez, saddled his horse one morning before dawn and rode away without a word.

• • •

Three days after Martínez left, the sun reappeared, its light and warmth welcome sensations. Feeling disjointed, unconnected, uncertain, I stood shirtless in the direct light for over an hour, letting the rays heat my body. I hoped for restoration, for some sense of purpose and direction.

The wind picked up, carrying a burden of yellow sand and dust from the desert below. The wind and its load overtook me as I saddled my horse to ride along the stream bank near camp in search of wild onions and garlic. I hoped for the chance to bag a few rabbits for the evening meal.

Rather than curse the wind and the sand, I felt an odd affection for it. It sang to me. I dismounted and walked a few paces from the gray and stood facing the breeze, meeting the sand and dust head-on, taking pleasure in the sound of the grains striking the legs of my pantalones, the feel of the wind's embrace, the sound of its song.

I had heard this song before, but this time the voice was different. This time it was the voice of El Enano—distant, muffled, but recognizable.

It sang, "*Vaya cuando puedes.*"

Go while you can.

The Parting

La Separación

I don't know how I knew I was ready to leave, I only knew the time had come.

The new voice in the wind was telling me to go, but I sensed others were also calling me back toward the border. Perhaps I missed my mother, my brother and sister; perhaps I worried about them. Perhaps I worried about myself, about my willingness to stay when I knew I was weary of the turmoil and heartsick at the destruction, the killing, the injustices, the sadness. The loss. We fought the devil but we couldn't beat him.

The only real happiness I had known was while working alongside la gente of pueblo San Benito, helping them to rebuild their town and their lives.

Chávez knew it was time also. I never told him of my plan to leave, of what I was thinking, but one morning he saddled the gray I had been riding, the one with the coarse, bristly hair like its wild ancestors, the one that had ridden into many battles with me. Behind the cantle he tied a small pack containing some dried meat and tortillas. Chávez, knowing I could depend on the caballo, handed me the reins and said only, "*Buen viaje y vaya con Dios.*" Then, he turned away, walked back through the herd, and disappeared into the dark canyon.

The Head of a Virgin

La Cabeza de una Virgen

On the second day of my return journey, I was struck with a fever and a deep aching in every muscle. With great effort I made myself ride, stopping often near streams where I bathed my burning face and body and rested in cool shade where I could find it. Travel was slow and painful as I labored to stay in the saddle. Sweat poured from my body and chills racked my bones. The throbbing in my head made me believe I might be going mad, that I could be dying. I was still days, weeks, from the Río Grande.

Weak and unable to concentrate, I reined up in a small copse of robles, dismounted clumsily, untied my pack from the back of the saddle, and passed out in the shade of one of the trees.

Hours later, I woke from a terrifying dream, one filled with images of Herrera and El Enano. I looked for the gray, but he was gone. I tried to stand, only to fall back to my hands and knees. I tried to call out, but my parched throat yielded no sound, only grating pain. My skin burned with a heat I'd never experienced.

Now, certain I was dying, I crawled around in the dirt until I regained my sheltered spot under the roble. Crying, I passed again into a fevered, troubled sleep.

• • •

When I woke again I was on a pallet in a small, darkened room. Dazed and weak, my throat dry, cracked, and aching, I looked around and saw only an adobe shell sparsely furnished with crude chair and table and a few Catholic icons hanging from the walls.

The largest, a cruelly battered and bloody Christ hanging from a cross, stared down at me.

Weaving in and out of consciousness, blurred images passed before my fogged eyes, images coming and going, images I thought were angels. I had a sense of a female presence, a clean smell somewhere out in the smoky darkness of the room, a movement like shadows inside a crystal.

In my half sleep and confusion I believed I had died and by some miracle found myself on the threshold of someone else's notion of heaven.

A sweet voice sang softly above my head, and a spoonful of warm broth was introduced into my mouth. As I lay on the pallet breathing heavily from the exertion of eating, a moist, cool cloth governed by a gentle touch washed my brow, my face, my neck, my chest. As my eyes focused, I saw a woman, one with a distinct Indian character to her features, a young woman who smiled as she ministered to me.

I watched her shadowy form as she silently walked around the room, moving with grace, almost like a dancer. Her long, dark hair flowed, waved behind her. She had long bones for an Indian.

The woman sensed me watching her and turned to meet my gaze. She placed a hand to my forehead and said, "The fever has broken."

Then she held my hand.

With difficulty, I asked, "My horse?"

"No horse was near you when you were found by my brother and uncle," she said.

"Where am I?"

"Piedras Negras."

"How long have I been here?"

"Four days."

• • •

Another day passed before I could stand, and even that effort forced me to lean against the wall for support. I grew hoarse thanking my caregiver.

She only smiled and said, "I am glad you are alive."

The following morning I ventured outside the small adobe and into a village of about sixty souls, all going about their daily chores, children and elderly alike, each nodding and waving, each smiling as if they were glad I was among them.

Near the center of the village stood the church, a rock, adobe, and wattle structure that could hold the entire population of the village within its walls and likely did so every Sunday and holy day. The priest, cassocked in black cotton, strode past with an air of arrogance in startling contrast to la gente: they were thin, wiry, and muscular from their hard work in the fields; he was portly and soft-fleshed from the absence of physical labor.

He was the only one in the pueblo who did not greet me with a smile.

• • •

Two days later, feeling stronger, I walked to the closest field where half a dozen campesinos hoed peppers, calabazas, and beans. I spotted my young caretaker working in the rows alongside the men, chopping weeds from between the plants, kneeling now and then to groom one of the pepper plants. Her long, crow-black hair reflected the sunlight. Her features were soft, her skin smooth. The lights in her startling black eyes sparkled and danced. She was beautiful.

At my approach, she smiled, dropped her hoe on the ground, and placed a hand on my forehead, then both hands on my face.

"You are well," she said. "I am so glad."

Our eyes held for several seconds, then her smile broadened and she said, "I am María. And you?"

"Carlos," I said.

María introduced me to her brother, Roberto, and her uncle, Gustavo, the men who found me and carried me to Piedras Negras, the village named after the dark lava rock that dominated the landscape. The men shook my hand vigorously and slapped me on the back, each expressing satisfaction and delight that I had survived.

Gustavo was older. Though browned, bent, and wrinkled from working a lifetime in the fields, his eyes twinkled with the joy of living. Roberto was shorter, squat, and muscular, with a round, youthful face and bowl-cut hair.

I looked around. Extensive fields of corn, beans, peppers, and squash stretched out lush and green. Children played in the nearby slow-moving river where women filled metal buckets and gourds with water.

"Paradise," I muttered.

"*Sí*," María said, "*paraíso*, except when we are visited by hacendado Mueller's raiding vaqueros."

I flinched at the mention of the name and stared hard at the ground, thinking of El Enano. María sensed my discomfort and placed a hand on my arm, a gentle touch.

"You know of hacendado Mueller?"

"*Sí*," I said, but chose to explain nothing.

I picked up María's hoe and took a place in the field, chopping weeds from between the plants. Later, I carried water to the adobe and split firewood. It felt good to be working. I felt strong, stronger than I had in weeks. I also felt a new and strange kind of contentment.

That night, María walked with me along the bank of the river. She told me stories of the land, of her people. She related tales handed down over generations, tales of gods and gold, of flood and drought, of harvest and celebration, of fear and fighting. I listened, enraptured, for hours as she unfolded the history of her ancestors and how they loved this land, embraced it, settled it, cultivated it, prayed over it, and sometimes died for it.

• • •

María approached me near the tiny plaza the next afternoon and touched me lightly on my forearm. Her eyes, large and black, shiny as the surface of a lake on a quiet moonlit night, showed no little concern. Her hair—long, clean, and shiny—hung to her waist. Barefooted, graceful, and lovely, she wore only a thin, white, handmade cotton shift.

"I heard Mueller's vaqueros are close to the village," she said. "I am a virgin. I do not want to die."

I did not understand.

"I want a son," she said, "one that will look like you, but with coppery skin like me. I have been watching you, studying you closely from the time you were brought to the village."

I did not know what to say.

"There is a rock house in the foothills," she said, pointing toward the west. "It is abandoned. Will you meet me there?"

• • •

I arrived an hour past sundown. She stood in the doorway of the stone shelter, a candle burning on the floor behind her, her shift transparent in the dim backlighting. I had never seen anything so lovely.

She took my hand and led me inside to sit by the candle on a soft woven mat. We talked of little things, about some of la gente in Piedras Negras, about the weather. She asked me where I came from, asked me why I was here. She handed me a fresh apricot from the small orchard behind the church. She made me laugh.

Then, growing serious, she said, "According to the campesinos and vaqueros alike, the head of a virgin is a powerful talisman. They believe such a charm protects them from evil and death, and they carry the heads into battle in saddle-hung pouches in the hope they will be protected. The vaqueros who ride for the hacendados, most of them former campesinos themselves, even steal the heads of virgins from fresh graves. Young girls are taken from their villages and beheaded."

She tilted her perfect head and smiled a sad smile. Her teeth gleamed in the moonlight that filtered through the open window. From somewhere in the night, breaking the silence, an owl called from a great height.

Flushed from her lilting voice and sweet smell, I watched as she arched backward on the mat. She raised her arms, reaching for me, and drew me down.

I started to tell her about my uncertainty, my inexperience, but she interrupted me and said, "Not tonight, but soon. For now kiss me. Just kiss me."

The Bath

El Baño

Following a day of working in the fields, it became my habit to bathe in the river. I liked to lie in the water at the edge of the current and let the cool flow wash away the day's grime, the fatigue of honest toil. I would remain thus sometimes for more than an hour contemplating the months with Chávez, contemplating San Lorenzo, San Benito, Piedras Negras, contemplating a future.

One evening as I walked toward the river, María intercepted me and took my hand.

"Come," she said, and led me to a steep bank one hundred yards downstream from the village, showing me a spring where fresh water gushed out of the exposed bedrock and collected in a shallow pool.

"Here," she said, "is where I and the other women come to wash our hair and bathe while the men lave themselves in the silty brown water of the river upstream."

A small leather pack hung from one shoulder. Pointing to it, I said, "What's in there?"

"Shhh," she said, holding a finger to her lips. She searched through the bag and withdrew a shredded yucca root.

"*Jabón*," she said. Soap.

Without pausing, she removed my boots, my camisa, then my pantalones, and playfully pushed me into the pool until I stood under the flow of the spring. Self-conscious, I covered myself with my hands.

Laughing, she ignored my shyness and worked the yucca root between her hands until it yielded rich and fragrant suds. Standing on her toes, she reached up and washed my hair, which was overlong and renegade from months of neglect. After rinsing my head, she turned her attention to my neck, arms, torso, legs, and feet. She scrubbed and scrubbed until I thought my skin would pull loose from the meat. Then, giggling, she rinsed me off.

The water soaked her thin cotton shift and it clung to her flesh like a second, transparent skin. The muscles in her rounded buttocks danced as she moved. Her breasts strained at the cloth. Her enlarged, dark nipples were taut beneath the fabric.

Feelings I had never before experienced or understood swept over and embarrassed me as I grew hard and erect.

María rinsed me, turning me around twice under the fall of the water, and left me with my back to her. When I heard another giggle, I turned to find her standing naked in front of me, her wet shift tossed onto the bank. She stood poised as if sculpted from stone, each curve of shoulder, hip, and breast perfect, as if ordained by the gods. When she embraced me, the breath left my trembling body.

Her eyes never leaving mine, her smile never leaving her face, María bathed herself. After rinsing, she took my hand and led me to a grassy spot where she had spread a soft, blue cotton serape.

She knelt and whispered, "Now, it is right."

Sighing, she guided me down onto her body as moonlight poured through the cottonwood trees.

The Blood of María

El Sangre de María

Midafternoon of the next day, I was walking side by side with María in the cornfield. Overhead, two crows flew high toward the northwest, issuing raucous cawing as they went. I shielded my eyes against the sun and watched them disappear beyond the far trees.

"Crows are bad luck," said María.

A moment later, a young boy ran to the edge of the cornfield screaming, "They are coming! They are coming!"

Beside me, Gustavo muttered a curse, threw down his hoe, and hastened to his adobe. María, working several rows over, sped to the youngster and spoke with him for a moment. Returning to my side, she explained that the vaqueros were coming, and they were looking for the gringo youth they heard was living in Piedras Negras, the gringo who rode with Chávez, who stole their cattle and horses, the *norteamericano* who whipped and killed their compañeros.

"I must leave," I said to María.

"No," she replied. "You would not have a chance on the road. Remain here."

She turned and walked back to the edge of the field to meet the riders who thundered up the trail.

There were seven of them, each wearing full bandoleras, each carrying revolvers and rifles and machetes, each intent on killing. I eyed them through tall stalks of the end-of-season corn, but they could not see me.

The riders reined up in front of María, horses blowing, saddles creaking. The leader barked a question at María, who shrugged her shoulders and pointed away from the village toward the north. He said something else and the others broke into laughter while they spurred their prancing mounts into a circle around her.

With a quick motion, the leader reached down and grabbed a fistful of María's hair, pulling her up on her toes and screaming words at her I could not understand. I grabbed the hoe and started forward when Gustavo, just returned from his casa with a pistola in his hand, tackled me from behind and threw me to the ground. I tried to rise, but Gustavo, then Roberto, were on top of me, pinning me to the soil.

Gustavo whispered, "The vaqueros are looking for you. They intend to kill you. María has told them you left the village days ago. They do not believe her."

We peered through the rows of cornstalks, catching only brief glimpses of María and the vaqueros. One of the riders dismounted, stepped toward her, and tore away her blouse and then her skirt. Again, I fought to rise, but Gustavo and Roberto held me fast.

"Don't be a fool," Roberto said. "They might kill us all."

"Be quiet. They might leave," Gustavo said, hissing.

María slapped the vaquero across the face and the others laughed at this. Enraged, he struck her hard on the side of her head and she went down.

María's screams rent the afternoon air, and the harsh laughter of the vaqueros grew louder. Horses skittered, left the circle, then returned. For a moment, I saw María on the ground, a vaquero on top of her, two others holding her legs apart, the rest cheering, yelling encouragement, and unbuckling their belts.

As María's frantic voice rose, I fought hard against the grasp of the two men, thrashing wildly as they kept their weight on me, kept me tight to the ground. Gustavo placed his lips close to my ear and ordered, "Stop. You can do nothing. María bleeds for you."

Then he slammed the butt of the pistola against my head, dropping me into stillness.

• • •

I awoke to gunfire, to the mad galloping of horses, to the screams of la gente. Rising to my knees in the field, I saw María's body on the ground where the vaqueros left her. She was covered in blood.

Turning toward the village, I stood in motionless shock at what I saw.

Vaqueros raced their horses through and around the village, back and forth across the tiny plaza in front of the church. Two of them had removed their saddles and rode bareback, demonstrating their skills to one another and to the terrified villagers by riding backward, by hanging under their mounts, by jumping off and leaping astride again. One stood balanced on his caballo's back as the mount galloped through the streets of the pueblo.

Two of the riders set fire to the houses constructed of river cane and juniper, the hellish crackling sound of the burning wood reaching my ears.

An old man tried to hobble out of the way of one of the mounted vaqueros only to be ridden down and left lying motionless in the dust.

Another campesino, attempting to save a few possessions from his burning house, was cut down with a machete in front of his wife and children.

Two vaqueros, laughing and cursing, pulled a naked woman from her house. As one held her legs apart, the other lowered his pants, mounted her, and brutally raped her as he slapped her over and over across the face.

Pulled from her hiding place behind some wooden crates, a thirteen-year-old girl was dragged to the center of the plaza. In seconds her clothes were torn away and two men raped her, calling for others to join them. When she would not stop screaming, they bludgeoned her until she was quiet. And still.

Another vaquero, Neanderthal-like with thick eyebrows growing as one, exited an adobe carrying a very young girl over his shoulder. When the father of the screaming child clutched at the captor's arm, begging him for mercy, he was shot between the eyes. The vaquero pulled the dress from the little girl and placed her belly-down atop a barrel. As he raped her, the mother ran screaming from the house and began beating him with a shovel handle. Turning from the child, the vaquero faced the mother, pulled the piece of wood from her grasp, and slammed it across her face. As she lay unconscious on the ground, he raped her also.

A man of twenty was roped, tied to a fence post, and lashed with a bullwhip, three vaqueros taking turns, each one trying to inflict greater pain and damage than the previous. One of them, tiring of the game, walked up to the semiconscious man and shot him through the head.

As I watched in stomach-tightening despair, the world started closing in, my vision narrowed, gray speckles formed and floated before my eyes. I wanted to run to the fight, wanted to turn the attention of the blood-maddened riders toward me. I wanted to kill them all, but my legs wouldn't move. Instead, I collapsed as if the ground had opened up to swallow me.

• • •

I stumbled dazed through the village at dusk, currents of gun smoke and dust not yet settled still in the air.

Fourteen dead, the rest ruined. Tears coursed down my face, carving tiny rivulets through the crusted dirt from the field, tears that struck the ground, making audible plopping sounds.

Passing the hand-dug well in the center of the plaza, I saw a body floating within, its drained blood mixing with the water and turning it crimson.

I walked into the ransacked church. The chalices and crosses of gold and silver had been carried away by the raiders. There, spread-eagled on the floor in cruciform, was the priest, his body riddled by dozens of bullets, a wide puddle of coppery-smelling blood radiating beneath him. Two pigs were feasting on his flesh.

The following morning, just after sunrise, Gustavo, Roberto, and I buried María on the tiny hillside campo santo beside her deceased relatives. I dug the hole with my bare hands, removing the sand and dirt and gravel until striking bedrock three feet below. With bleeding fingers, I wrapped her in her blue serape, the same one on which we had lain. I held her close, rocking her, stroking her hair, not wanting to give her up. When I had cried myself dry, I parted the serape and placed a kiss on her bruised forehead. Exhausted, trembling, I placed her into the grave and refilled it. For hours I carried rocks and piled them atop the mound. I kept busy, trying to distract my thoughts from my own guilt, from my own culpability for not saving her, from my own great loss.

Somehow I found more tears. After the others returned to the village, I sat at the foot of the grave and cried again for María, cried for the village, paraíso. Paradise.

Then, I cried for myself.

At sundown, Gustavo and Roberto came to the campo santo, pulled me away from the grave, and led me back to the wounded and scarred pueblo.

• • •

By the time the sun rose the next day I was several miles north of Piedras Negras. Drained from the previous day's nightmare, weary from not sleeping, weary from thinking, and exhausted from shouldering an unbearable burden of guilt, I began walking toward the border.

María had become part of me. I knew I would never again cross the plains without feeling the sun of her smile or the welcome rain of her touch. I knew I would never see a newborn child without thinking of her wanting a son. I knew I would never be near a fire when its sparks would not ignite a memory of her laughter. I knew I had never felt such sadness, such a loss that hurt deep to the core of my bones. I had never known true beauty until I saw her, and I had never known my own heart until I touched her.

Now, without her, as I trudged toward the Río Grande, still many miles, many days away, I wondered who and what I would be when I crossed back to the other side.

The Savior

El Salvador

Days, maybe weeks, later and still miles from the border, I passed through a long, wide valley called Agua de Medicina—Medicine Water—as sunset overtook me. My eyes, red and raw, watered from the persistent desert winds that traveled with me.

Dispirited, bone-weary from the endless days of walking, tired of the incessant, sand-laden wind, I wrapped myself in my serape and fell asleep on the lee side of a thick roble. Throughout the night, dreams ravaged my slumber, dreams of blood and fighting, tearing me sharply from rest and recovery. By morning I was exhausted and dreading another long day of travel. By the end of the day, I knew I would be dreading the night—and the dreams.

I rose, stretching stiffness from my limbs, filling my lungs with the cool morning air. My eyes still burned, and I wasn't looking forward to more days of walking.

An unexpected voice startled me, and I spun on my heels to see a smiling, smooth-skinned face belonging to man in his late fifties. His short, squat, muscular body identified him as an Indian. His manner of dress suggested he was more prosperous than most of the indios who lived in the region. His face and demeanor communicated friendliness, welcome.

"Hungry?" he asked.

"I am."

"You know horses?"

"Some."

"Can you break the wild ones and train them to the saddle?"

"I can," I lied.

"Then," he said, "I can offer you a hot meal this morning and a job for two weeks. The pay is good, but the food is better."

He grinned and continued. "I am Santos." He held out his hand and I shook it.

He motioned for me to follow, and we walked several yards to where his horse was tied. He mounted, assisted me to a position behind him, and together we rode to his rancho on the floor of the valley a mile away.

Following a meal of eggs, tortillas, chiles, chorizo, and thick, sugar-laced coffee, we walked to the barn, and he showed me which saddle to use on a bay mare in the corral.

Pointing eastward, Santos said, "Ride to the flats next to the river below the mesa and bring in the wild ones. There were twenty-one of them the last time I visited. All good, spirited, all capable of making fine mounts."

A woman, surely a daughter, not a wife, entered the barn and regarded me with curiosity. Unlike her father, she was tall, lithe, and beautiful, and garbed in riding breeches and boots and a white camisa. Santos introduced us.

She smiled at me and politely said, "*Buenos días.*"

Santos looked at her proudly and said, "Sunflower, ride with him and show him the way. You can be back by nightfall."

Behind the woman strode a man, his eyes suspicious and hostile. He was introduced as her brother, Esteban. He was dressed in black—pantalones, camisa, boots, even hat. Esteban swaggered, a practiced bravado, thrusting out his chest and peering down his hawklike nose. Surly, he said nothing to me, ignored my outstretched hand, and turned away to whisper into Santos's ear, his palm resting on the butt of a revolver seated in a black holster. A moment later he swung toward me, contempt percolating in the dark pupils, his eyes settling on my torn and ragged clothes. As he glared, I stared back, refusing to avert my gaze.

• • •

Sunflower saddled a spirited Appaloosa while I tightened the cinch on my mare. After stuffing two metal canteens into saddlebags, we rode away toward the mesa. Behind us in the northwest, clouds built, darkened, threatened, and the first drops from the storm struck as we entered the flats.

The wild horses, oblivious to the impending downpour, continued to graze at the far end of the large meadow, grinding silica-laden blades and stems between strong jaws. From a distance they were as much a part of the landscape as the rocks and trees.

Sunflower watched me study the horses as the skies opened and the rain fell in sheets. Heeling her horse to the front to get my attention, she pointed to a large overhang in a nearby cliff face and led me away from the storm. Drenched, we guided our mounts into the sheltered space, the clicking of shod hooves on the bare rock in counterbeat to the thunder overhead and the raindrops pelting the dry soil. We removed the saddles, brushed down the horses' backs with our gloved hands, and left them ground-hitched against the back wall. I found scattered wood within the shelter and gathered some for a fire.

We sat side by side in silence next to the little blaze and watched the storm, watched the wild ones in the distance. Shivering, Sunflower crossed her arms over her breasts and huddled close to herself. I looked at her fingers—long, delicate, strong. Her dark eyes reminded me of agates when she turned to look at me, a smile hesitant on her lips.

"I'm cold," she whispered, and moved closer.

Wordless, we sat. Stiff and unresponsive, my mind and body were shut inside the tight shell I'd constructed to keep myself together.

"You are called Carlos, correct?" she asked.

"Yes."

"My name is Girasol, which means Sunflower in my language. My father calls me Sunflower when Anglos come to the rancho. He thinks it is polite to do so."

"Girasol," I said without looking up. "It's a pretty name."

"What's wrong, Carlos? You seem to have misery bound tightly inside you."

Her simple words served as a key that unlocked the hasp on my heart.

I could not speak for several minutes, then, shaking, I whispered, "They raped her. Killed her. I could do nothing. They ruined *la gente*; they ruined the village."

"Who?" Girasol asked. "Where?"

Unable to contain any of it, the words poured out of me in hot, weeping torrents, like molten lava from a rent in the earth's crust.

When I finished, Girasol lowered her face to her bent knees in silent, unmoving thought.

When I could speak no more, I started shaking. Before I could stop them, tears formed, the burning drops growing in both eyes, spilling over and running down my face. I held my head and sobbed, my shoulders racking in rhythm.

Later, when I could cry no more, I raised my head and looked at Girasol just inches away. She had not moved. She felt me watching her and she glanced up. Smiling, she reached around me, pulled me closely into her arms, and rocked me lightly. I could smell the flowery scent of the flesh at her neck, feel the damp wetness of her loose hair. For a long, long time, until the tension seeped out of my body, she held me.

• • •

The darkness deepened. The storm raged on. Lightning crashed, shaking the rock face of the mesa, startling the horses into a quickstep dance on the stone floor. Still, all I heard was her breath. All I felt was her mouth, her body shivering under mine, her touch given like a gift, her love a miraculous saving grace.

• • •

One of the horses nickered me awake to clear skies and the fresh smell of the rain-soaked meadow. Girasol, beautiful and smiling, coaxed the embers of the previous night into a small fire. I thought about her compassion, our desire. I thought about Santos and how I loved him for taking me, a poor gringo, into his home. I thought about the brother and the way he regarded me with pure hatred.

Sunflower sighed and said, "They will be out looking for us by now. My father will be very worried, perhaps angry."

"Your brother, he will kill me," I said.

I gathered her into my arms, and we sat by the flames, holding each other.

"I am grateful to your father for helping me," I said. "I would like to repay him with work. It's all I have."

"There is nothing you can do," she said. "I must go now, and go quickly. You must leave this place at once before Esteban arrives."

I saddled the horses as she straightened her hair and pulled on her boots. I helped her mount, handing her the reins to the bay mare.

"You have saved me," I said.

She leaned over and touched my face, then gigged her gelding into a trot. As she rode away, she turned and shouted back, "Don't follow. I hope I see you again, but for now *buen viaje*."

I stood shaking under the lip of dripping rock and watched as she galloped across the meadow, stirring the wild ones into flight. In one rushing, blurred vision of suspended movement, they disappeared from view.

The Return

La Vuelta

Even before I saw the river, I smelled it, the powerful familiarity of its moist, earthy aroma and the scent-rich salt cedars growing along the bank invading my senses. I knew if I left this place for fifty years, then returned, blindfolded, I would know the river, would still know this precise spot. Birds and fish somehow return to the places they were born, come back to lay eggs and hatch out their young, giving rise to new life. Would there be new life for me?

I heard the gurgle of the river before I spotted its shimmering surface, heard the wind that whirled above it. I knew exactly where I was. I recognized the song of the wind near the crossing.

I had been gone for nine months, maybe ten. I ached with anticipation and dread, afraid of what I might find or not find, afraid of who I was, concerned about what I might have become.

The sky was overcast and gray as I walked the final mile to the river. The wind gusted and slow, heavy drops of rain fell, singularly and far apart, a hint and promise of more to come. I pulled the battered sombrero that Chávez had given me down tight to keep it from blowing away. The soles of my riding boots were paper-thin, with holes in places where the cold seeped through, and, inside, the soles of my feet were sore and torn. Stained with blood that never washed out, my campesino camisa and pantalones, now little more than rags hanging from my frame, were held together by the barest of threads. My serape, filthy and ripped, was all that protected me from the biting January air.

On reaching the southern bank of the river, I stood, leaning against the wind, and watched the red-brown water. Across the Río Grande, the familiar álamo with its spreading limbs sheltered the tiny marker I'd placed on Pete's grave so long ago. The air turned colder, chilling me with an attack on my flanks.

Sitting at the river's edge, I pulled off the ruined boots, threw them into the current, and watched as they tumbled and sank. Weary, I made myself stand and pulled off my tattered shirt and pants, balled them up, and gave them to the water also. They followed the path of the boots and disappeared below the surface.

From my pack I retrieved my old denim pants, shirt, and jacket, and put them on. At the bottom of the pack, the revolver, still loaded, nested tightly in the holster wrapped by the gun belt. I pulled the bundle out into the daylight and stared at it for a long time. Fingering the butt of the gun, I tugged it from its leather casing and held it, caressing it as I would a woman I had longed for.

I became lost in the dreams again, dreams that carried me away to frightening places, places where I had searched for myself and found things that caused me to grow wary and cautious. I found places that stirred the dormant pain in my heart back to life, and tears began to flow as the rain fell harder.

Particles of sand stirred by the rising wind stung my wet face and brought me back. I slipped the revolver into the holster, placed it back inside the pack, closed it, and tied it tightly. Standing, I whirled the pack above my head and hurled it into the river, impressed with the mighty splash.

I felt for the knife hanging from the leather thong around my neck. I thought to throw it away too, but something stayed the impulse. Holding the knife, a strange calm settled over me, and I heard distant voices asking me to return, calling me back to the Sierra Madres.

Then there was nothing. Nothing but the wind.

I scanned the sky, the fast approaching storm on the horizon, and calculated that a half hour of daylight remained, time enough to cross the river and walk through the fields and canebrake to my mother's house before dark. I hesitated only a moment, then stepped into the cold water, the rough gravel sharp on my bare feet. The current tugged at my legs and the wind threatened to unbalance me. Unsteady, I waded carefully into deeper water.

Without warning, I stepped into a hidden hole and went down and under. I thrashed my way back to the surface, coughing and spitting out muddy water just in time to watch my sombrero float away, snatched from my head by the current. I braced myself against the flow, water lapping at my thighs, and followed the progress of the large hat until it disappeared around a bend.

Soaked and tired, muddied from chest to toes, I crawled up the opposite bank and, pausing to smell and taste the Texas air, I turned and looked back to the south. In the growing darkness, the cross on the roof of the church in the village beyond the floodplain, beyond the line of cottonwoods, appeared burnished. Tilted slightly, it listed like the mast of a sinking ship. Though thick, scudding clouds obscured the setting sun, the cross reflected back a carmine hue.

In the nebular gloom, I leaned, dripping, against the rough bark of the álamo to catch my breath before walking on. Sensing I was not alone, I jerked to an alert, defensive posture, reached for the knife, and found myself face to face with the goatherd.

He smiled, his eyes crinkling, his teeth gleaming, the scar on his cheek stark in the fading light. He reached out a gnarled hand, and his long, leathery fingers lightly touched my face. I did not flinch or move away.

"I prayed for your safe return," he said.

I did not know what to say.

For long moments he stared across the river into the distance, then turned back to me.

"Did you fly with the eagles?"

At first I could not speak. Then, finally, I replied, "*Sí*, I did."

He smiled again, clasped my shoulder, and disappeared with the wind into the night.

Home

La Casa

A long, yellow rectangle of light from the kitchen window stretched out from the otherwise darkened casa like a welcoming embrace. I stood for a moment in the warm glow and watched my mother inside cleaning some after-dinner spots from the old, chipped gas range. Somewhere, from the other end of the house, I could hear my brother and sister playing. It was easy to smile, easy to feel good about being home.

Rounding the corner of the old stone house, I opened the front door, stepped into the living room, and said, "Mom."

Something clattered to the kitchen's linoleum floor.

"Carlos? Carlos!"

My mother rushed into the room and flipped on a light switch, wiping her hands on the frayed, purple-iris print apron that covered her faded cotton dress.

"Where have you been?" she asked, tears welling up in her eyes. "I've been worried sick. I've called the sheriff so many times, had him looking high and low for you. He said you probably went to California like so many others are doing these days. I was worried you were dead."

"I've been in Mexico," I answered.

She placed her hands on my shoulders, held me at arm's length, and looked me up and down, appraising me. Then she clutched me tightly in an embrace that took the air from my lungs.

"Look at you! Are you all right? You've filled out. Your skin is darker. What were you doing? Look at your clothes. They are in tatters, little more than filthy rags! Where are your boots? I paid good money for those boots. Were you in jail? Your hair is so long."

"I'm fine. I've been working," I said. "I was far from any telephones and couldn't call."

"And your eyes," she said, with a look of pain. "What has happened to your eyes? They seem darker. You look mean, troubled."

"I'm OK," I said with a deep sigh.

She wrapped her arms around me again, her cheek pressed to mine as I bent down to hug her in return. As she patted my back, she said over and over again, "Oh Carlos, oh Carlos, oh Carlos." Her tears rushed out.

Realizing I was famished from days of little substantive food, I asked, "Do we have anything to eat?"

"I'll fix you something. Go see your brother and sister."

She hurried into the kitchen, the heels of her shoes clicking on the scratched and torn linoleum.

Michael, twelve, and Dianne, sixteen, were sitting cross-legged on the floor of my old bedroom playing a card game. I leaned against the doorjamb and watched them fuss at each other.

"You cheated."

"Did not."

"Did so."

"You looked at my cards when I went to the bathroom."

"Did not."

During a brief lull in their squabble, I said, "Hi."

They looked up, shocked, then crawled to their feet and ran to hug me. They asked questions about where I'd been, what I'd been doing, but I evaded them and told them how glad I was to see them.

After a few minutes, Michael heaved a deep sigh and said, "Will I have to give up your bedroom? Mom said I could use it."

"He can't move back into my room," Dianne insisted.

"It's not necessary," I said to Michael. "I'll bunk on the couch for now."

The homecoming visit with my sister and brother lasted several more minutes. The relaxed small talk and unimportant news of neighbors and friends made me feel like I had only been away for a few days instead of almost a year. Our conversation was interrupted when my mother called from the kitchen, inviting me to come and eat.

On the way to the kitchen I passed by the bathroom. I stepped inside and looked in the mirror. The face I saw frightened me. The beard, the dark skin. Were those lines running along the outside of my eyes? From squinting so much in the sun, I thought.

It was the eyes that held my attention again—dark eyes that seemed like deep, black pools with no bottom. *These are not my eyes*, was my first thought. Then, *how did I get these eyes?*

I walked back through the living room looking at the old furniture, the small collection of books on the bottom shelf of a two-shelf bookcase. On the wall above the bookcase hung a crucifix, the bleeding Christ bearing a look of agony.

Nothing had changed. Nothing at all.

My mother set two grilled cheese sandwiches on a plate and put them on the table along with a glass of iced tea. As I ate, she peppered me with questions to which I gave cryptic responses. Frustrated, she turned to admonitions.

"Why didn't you tell me where you were going?" she asked, her faced creased in stern tightness. "You didn't even leave me a note. Is that how a son treats his own mother? Why didn't you write me a letter, let me know you were OK? How many rosaries did I have to say? How many nights did I lie awake worrying, praying for you? You have no idea what you have put me through. Don't ever do this to me again, do you hear me?"

She started crying again.

"I know you've been in some kind of trouble," she said. "I see it in your eyes. Your eyes are so . . . so hard. You never used to look that way." She dabbed at tears in her own eyes with the corner of her apron.

When I didn't reply, she got up from the table and took a dollar bill from her purse.

"Here," she said. "Tomorrow, you go get a haircut. I won't have you living in this house looking like that, like a Mexican."

I tried to distract her with a question. "How are Johnny Red, Floyd, and J. Clovis?"

"They stay busy worrying their mothers like you worry me."

"Are they still around?"

"Sure. Still cowboying, rodeoing, getting into trouble and fights like before. They have no sense of what is important. They need to get jobs, settle down, get married."

"They're just trying to squeeze some living out of life before they decide on a career," I said.

"If you stay here, you have to shave that face and get a haircut."

"So, you don't mind if I stay here for a while?" I asked.

"No, not if you help out like before. There are chores needing done. This house needs repairs. You will have to get a job."

She broke down, buried her face in her hands, and tried to keep me from seeing her weeping. "We don't have any money," she cried.

"No problem. I'll get work in a few days. Everything will be OK."

I could tell by the look on her face that my father hadn't been around for a long time.

The Killers

Los Asesinos

Within the week, I was back at my old job on the loading docks. On weekends, I was able to book some fights in Juárez, Las Palomas, Zaragoza, and San Elizario. I remained for a few months until I found day work on several different ranches in the county. Because I showed up early, worked hard, and stayed late, I earned a reputation as a dependable employee. The ranch owners appreciated me because I was quiet, never complained, and went about the chores of tending cattle and horses and repairing windmills without complaint. They traded me around with each other as needs required. I liked the arrangement just fine since there was something different to do each day.

I liked it best when I was sent out alone to build or repair fence. Being on the range for days at a time gave me the solitude I craved. It provided time I needed to ponder the past, to think about the future. It gave me time to be alone, something I craved, needed. I reveled in the sweet peace of solitude, the only sounds the hissing of the windblown sand grains at my feet, the crunch of the posthole digger into the sandy, gravelly soil, the beat of hammering wire nails into the cedar fence posts.

It was enough to be safe, warm, and well fed. At night, when the dreams came over and over again, dreams of Tomasito, Herrera, El Enano, María, I knew that death had also become my close companion.

One April day, Uncle Charlie Duke, the manager of the Hueco Mountain Ranch, called me in from fencing to help with branding, tagging, and castrating calves. Uncle Charlie had been a cowman all his life, working on and managing ranches from Arizona to Texas. Old age had whitened his hair and added some pounds to his frame, and he smoked three or four packs of cigarettes a day, but he could still put in a full day's work, often outworking the hands. Though he wasn't related to anyone I knew, everyone called him Uncle Charlie.

I joined Charlie and six other men, all around his age, and together we herded the calves to the pen, roped and dragged them to the fire, branded, castrated, and tagged them, and doctored scrapes and cuts. It was hot, sweaty work made easier by the smooth-riding, muscled, experienced roan I rode. The horse seemed eager to contribute.

I watched the others as I worked. These men, unlike the Mexicans and indios I rode with only months earlier, rode, trained, and behaved around their horses as if they were afraid of them, as though they needed to be controlled, dominated. The Mexicans lived with their caballos as though they were family members. Their horses were never dominated so much as they were incorporated into the daily operations of ranch or farm, fed by hand sometimes, talked to as friends might talk with one another. When it came time to break a Mexican pony, it was mostly a matter of climbing onto its back and riding it. The horse, which was raised to know the rider was friendly and kind, had little desire to buck.

Twelve and a half hours of hard work in the West Texas sun found the job completed and our team of eight men thoroughly exhausted.

Three of them, neighboring ranchers, headed back to their homes, but Uncle Charlie invited the rest of us—Clifford Jenkins, Jap Childress, Sam Kincaid, and me—to share a steak and frijole dinner at his house.

I hesitated in accepting his offer and said, "I have a lot of fence to string in the morning. I need to head back out and get a good night's sleep."

"It's OK, Carlos," said Uncle Charlie. "You can sleep in the bunkhouse tonight and get a late start in the morning. My wife Clara will fix you breakfast before you ride out to the fence."

I nodded my head, washed up on the back porch, and joined the others at the plank table.

With the meal over, Uncle Charlie pulled out a deck of cards and passed around cigars. Since I cared little for playing and didn't smoke, I contented myself with nursing a glass of whiskey neat and listening to their conversations.

During the third hand of five-card stud, Jenkins tipped back his sweat-stained, rancher-style Stetson, took a sip of whiskey, and with a squint in his dark green eyes turned to Kincaid and asked in a lowered voice, "Sam, did you ever kill anybody when you were in the war?"

"I got a couple of Krauts once, Cliff," Sam answered. "Why do you ask?"

"No reason. Just wondered. Always wondered what it was like to kill a man."

Gray-bearded Jap Childress looked up and said, "I killed a man once."

"What for?" Clifford asked.

"It was a long time ago, and it was over a woman," Jap said, a faraway look veiling his eyes. He offered no further information, and no one asked.

Uncle Charlie, after making certain Clara was nowhere near, volunteered, "I shot a man once just to see what it felt like. It was during a fight, and anybody would have told you the man needed killing anyway. And you know what? It felt good."

Childress, Kincaid, and Jenkins all forced some nervous, strained laughter followed by an uncomfortable silence. I got the feeling they were wishing the subject hadn't been brought up.

The room became uncomfortably quiet, the only sounds the shuffling of feet and an occasional nervous clearing of a throat. Trying to regain the previous momentum, Jenkins turned to me and asked, laughing, "Carlos? Did you ever kill anybody?"

All four men stared hard at me, awaiting my reply. The only response they got was silence and dark eyes refusing to give in to their question. They quieted, with more nervous coughing and shuffling.

The room suddenly seemed too warm, too close. I tipped back my whiskey and drained the last sip from the glass. Someone's chair scraped backward on the rough wood floor. I looked up and saw Uncle Charlie holding the bottle of seven-year-old bourbon in his sunspotted, calloused hand, extending it toward me, a look of apology on his face.

"No thanks," I said.

I set my empty glass on the table, rose from the chair, and said, "I guess I'll head out to the fence early in the morning."

I closed the door carefully behind me and stood in a sheen of moonlight filtering through the willow trees onto the front porch. I waited until I heard their conversation resume, then I walked over to the truck for my bedroll. As I walked past the rock corral toward the bunkhouse, a horse snorted and I stopped just to listen to the caballos stirring in the night.

I didn't want to go to sleep. I feared the dreams.

The News

Las Noticias

One day during late autumn nine or ten months following my return from Mexico, Uncle Charlie sent me to Villa Acuña, across the river from Del Río, Texas, in the state of Coahuila, Mexico, to evaluate a small herd of wild Mexican horses. If they were healthy, and if there were no import constraints, he gave me the authority to make arrangements to purchase them for the ranch.

I stopped at a border café and bar in Del Río for an enchilada dinner. The low adobe structure was a popular spot patronized by businessmen, blue-collar workers, fishermen, hunters, and occasional tourists. As I waited for a table, a flirty Mexican waitress handed me a short glass of tequila. With a wink, she said, "Don't tell anyone. We are not supposed to serve liquor." I leaned against the counter and sipped the fermented agave.

Moments later I placed the empty glass next to the cash register. When I turned, the waitress was standing next to me, touching my arm, and inviting me to the booth at the back of the room. When I was seated, she handed me a menu.

I waved it away and said, "Green chile chicken enchiladas and iced tea, *por favor*."

She nodded and set down silverware and a paper napkin, gave me another smile, and left.

As I waited for my food, I picked up a newspaper from an adjacent table left behind by a previous diner. Some restless, wild thing clawed at my heart as I read the bold print headline:

Chávez Rides!

Ignoring the savory enchiladas, refried beans, rice, and iced tea, I read the article over and over. After months of harassing villagers unmolested, the vaquero militia commanded by a Sonoran hacendado with strong political connections was once again being met with violent opposition by a band of riders led by a man identified only as Chávez. According to the article, "The flanks of the Sierra Madres run red with the blood of vengeance."

Heart pounding, I finished my meal, paid, and stepped out into the Texas sunlight. A stiff breeze lifted a dirty-yellow haze of dust into the air. Squinting past the old pickups parked in a haphazard line along the front of the building, I studied the shimmering desert to the south beyond the Río Grande, beyond the Mexican town of Villa Acuña.

I walked to the riverbank and let the warm autumn night caress me. The wind picked up, coming from the south, its familiar voice singing once again: *Vaya cuando puedes.* Go while you can.

The Whorehouse

La Casa de Putas

This time I left a note for my mother on the kitchen table. Inside the folded paper I tucked my last fifty dollars. I'd spent the rest of my latest paycheck at a pawnshop in El Paso for a used Colt .45 and some ammunition.

This time, shouldering my pack and feeling for the knife hanging from my neck, I walked across the plank bridge that spanned the narrow, shallow Río Grande between El Paso and Ciudad Juárez.

I passed through Juárez and, on arriving at the southern edge of the city, thumbed a series of rides down the paved highway that ran to Ciudad Chihuahua, some 230 miles to the south, arriving the following afternoon.

I took up temporary residence at a hotel, the Blue Gardenia, which also served as a high-dollar whorehouse for wealthy Texans and Californians. The hotel was pricey for my thin wallet, but it was also a point through which most news of the region passed. Sooner or later someone would visit the Blue Gardenia who would know about the happenings in the sierras and perhaps know the whereabouts of Chávez.

During the day I searched the newspapers in hopes of finding some reference to Chávez. I listened to the gossip in the streets and slipped some pesos to those who traveled the foothills of the sierras, asking them to bring me information. But days turned into weeks with no reliable word. Occasionally I picked up day work on one of the nearby ranches, but mostly I earned some money by match-fighting in the plazas and palenques and betting on myself. Whenever I could convince one of the local boxing promoters to let me fight, I picked up more money in the arenas.

I made enough money to pay for the room and some good meals with a little to spare.

The hotel was clean, as clean as the finest inns in Ciudad Chihuahua, and the trio of daily meals served was prepared by one of the best chefs in Mexico. Tastefully decorated, the rooms were elegantly appointed with wallpaper, draperies, and furnishings imported from France and Italy.

The prostitutes were educated, poised, and polite. With great courtesy, they treated me like a close relative and saw to my needs. Each time I passed the women in the halls, they smiled and engaged me in conversation that entertained and delighted me. They treated me with dignity, and I responded in like manner.

One afternoon, sitting outside in the shade offered by the courtyard trees, I was reading a book when a young boy entered from the street through a wrought-iron gate and held out a stained piece of paper.

"Señor? Carlos del Santiago?"

"*Sí,*" I said.

"Geraldo told me to bring this to you."

"*Gracias,*" I said, and handed him a few centavos. "Tell Geraldo I will come by after the fight tonight."

"*Sí,* Señor," he responded, and walked back into the noisy street.

Scrawled in smeared pencil on the note were the words:

Piedras Negras is no more. Whereabouts of Chávez unknown.

Something snapped inside me. I folded the paper and used it to mark my place in my book, then rose from the chair.

One of the prostitutes, Carmen, was hanging clothes on the line. "You are going now?" she asked, a laundry basket perched on her sensuous hip.

"*Sí,*" I said.

"Will we see you any more?"

"Probably not," I answered.

"*Vaya con Dios, Señor*. The devil makes hard work for us, no?"

"Yes," I said, "he does."

The Bar

La Cantina

Not wishing to be seen or heard, I picked my way to the edge of the ragged little village called El Nido. La gente here knew me from times past, times of stolen horses, broken bones, bullet wounds. I knew that the vaqueros here had good memories, long ones. I moved with caution.

Dusk was beginning to settle around the sounds of laughter in the cantina—the clink of glasses, the disharmonious singing of the whores accompanied by the barking and wailing of dogs that roamed the muddy, manure-dotted streets. It was dangerous, but I was thirsty for drink, strong drink to wash away the dust and weariness of the long trail. Perhaps I might even overhear conversation pertaining to Chávez.

Or maybe I was thirsty for confrontation, thirsty for a return to battle. It had been almost a year, and some vital part of me had gone unchallenged for too long. Some part of me remained angry, unfulfilled. Some part of me craved revenge, justice.

Keeping to the darkness beside the buildings, I waited a long time in the shadows until the yellow-brown sun-glow faded into starlit night, then moved silently into the center of the village toward the cantina.

At that high altitude the air was cool, and I pulled my poncho tighter around my shoulders and lowered the battered sombrero I traded for in Chihuahua to hide my face. With the deep tan and the neglected beard and moustache, along with the worn and dirty clothes and boots, I looked much like any other transient campesino. I stepped from behind an adobe casa, crossed the dirt street, and entered the cantina.

All sound ceased and every man and woman turned to stare at me, a stranger. Harmless campesino, or an enemy? I could see the questions in their faces, could almost hear their minds turning with hesitation and wondering at whether or not this newcomer was one of Chávez's riders. Surely he would not be so foolish as to enter a cantina filled with vaqueros sworn to capture and kill him.

They regarded my torn pantalones and mud-covered boots, my weathered serape, my filthy sombrero with holes in the aged felt. They studied what little they could see of my deeply tanned, lined face and drooping moustache, my matted and grimy shoulder-length hair. They could see neither the revolver under the serape nor the cuchillo hanging from my neck.

Bowing my shoulders, I shuffled my way to the plank bar. While they listened intently, I murmured a request for mescal, using their mountain dialect.

A low murmur of conversation resumed. They must have satisfied their curiosity, accepted the fact that I was no threat, that I was simply an itinerant passing through, because they returned to their drinking, to their dice and bones, to their whores. Few regarded me any longer, content that I was little more than a poor traveler in poor clothes, something a dog might piss on and nothing more.

Most of them. My eyes scanned the room and settled on three men who still watched me intently from under the flat brims of their hats, dark eyes searching, probing, trying to pierce the cover of beard and dirt. I recognized them immediately as vaqueros who rode for hacendado Mueller. I remembered seeing them in Piedras Negras.

After downing a second mescal, I paid in pesos, pulled my sombrero low, and deliberately passed by the three, looking into the faces of each before walking out of the cantina into the night.

Without pausing, I hurried down the dirt road toward a trail that led to the barranca below, then switchbacked into the high sierras on the other side.

Let me pass through, I prayed, *just let me pass through so I can make it to Piedras Negras.* After traveling a hundred meters down the road, I heard the sound of a boot scraping gravel somewhere behind me. I turned to see the three men following, moving from one dark doorway to another.

They remembered me after all.

I ran my hand under the serape and along the heavy butt of the .45 tucked into my sash, the long barrel extending deep into my canvas pantalones.

A mile from the valley floor I heard them again, closer now. I paused in the shadowed shelter of the woods and watched them slipping from one tree to the next, trying to close the distance between us without being seen.

After several turns in the trail, nearing the bottom of the canyon where there were fewer rocks and the soil was mostly sand and silt, I stopped beside a thick álamo a few yards off the trail and pulled the .45 out into the cool night air. I checked to make certain there was a bullet in each of the six chambers, two for each man. I slipped the gun under the serape and hid myself behind the tree.

Now and again I heard the cracking of a twig, the soft padding of feet on the alluvial soil. Then they were past me, unaware that I had watched them as they had watched me in the cantina.

Why couldn't they have just let me pass?

I stepped out from behind the álamo holding the revolver close to my stomach under the cloth and called softly to them. Surprised, they wheeled around to face me. Their sudden, jerky movements as they tried to find me in the darkness made me smile.

"*¿Quién es?*" one of them whispered, as if the night demanded low voices.

"The one you seek, *cabrones*."

The tall one, the one with the bad teeth, the one Herrera told me always carried a long knife in the folds of his coat, stepped forward.

"*Pinche gringo*," he spat. "We knew it was you all along. We should have killed you with the others that time in Piedras Negras."

Raising the barrel of the revolver under the serape, I aimed at the forehead edge of his hat where the brim was illuminated by the beams of moonlight shooting through the branches of the tree.

"In some ways you did," I replied.

The tall one made a sudden move and the knife appeared in his hand, the blade rusted and jagged-edged. To his left, another movement, and the long-armed Indian boy pulled a machete from under his cape, the wide blade catching a glint of moonlight.

To the right, the third man, who remained still and grinned a toothless smile, said, "We mean to kill you this time, gringo! Tonight you will die."

The three lunged as one, knife and machete connecting with glancing blows, flashing disconnectedly in the lunar light. The front of my serape exploded as six rapid-fire shots destroyed the night stillness. Birds, startled from their slumber, fled the branches overhead as lead tore through muscle, tendon, bone.

I knew la gente from El Nido would come running to answer the call of gunfire, but they would not find me. They would only find what was left of their compañeros and wonder how and why they came to die. They would peer into the wooded canyon floor, trying to determine if a threat remained nearby. They would whisper the name Chávez over and over.

I took what little money I found in their pockets, threw their weapons into the underbrush, and, bleeding badly, limped away into the darker blackness of the barranca.

The Friends

Los Amigos

For weeks I searched the Chihuahuan countryside only to learn they were all gone. Too much time had passed, but here and there among the campesinos I still heard rumors, picked up pieces of gossip.

Olguín had been captured and hung by the vaqueros. Sánchez had been captured and shot by a firing squad. Borrego had been tortured, then crucified along the road to Boquillas. Escobar had been beheaded. Chávez had simply disappeared once again into the mountains and canyons of the sierras.

Now and then, according to whisperings in the pueblos, a lone warrior astride a streaking black caballo rode out of the night, coming to the aid of la gente, slaying or confounding the vaqueros.

I learned that old Jaramillo was in the jail at Camargo. I heard they made him mop the stones and concrete each day. I heard they cut out one of his eyes with the tip of a hot knife.

I went to see him. They made me wait two days.

When they finally let me in, he gripped me, hugging me tightly.

We both cried.

The Violation

La Violación

My dark hair grew long until it hung below my shoulders. Though I managed to scrape away my beard, I left the moustache, long and dangling. I acquired a rifle and a pair of bandoleras I wore across my chest. For weeks I went everywhere on foot until I wore out my boots. In a tiny *mercado*, I purchased a used pair of black, knee-high riding boots for a few pesos.

During a long trek through a portion of the Sierra Madres, I came upon a lone caballo grazing on the sweet grasses growing along the bank of a narrow stream. I squatted in the shade and watched the animal for a long time, admiring its sleek, black coat, the wiry muscles bunching and elongating beneath the skin. The frame and legs suggested some thoroughbred mixed with *mesteño.*

As if sensing it was being watched, the gelding raised its head and stared hard at me under the tree. Our eyes met and held for minutes. I rose and stepped out from under the shade. The black hesitated a moment, then walked purposefully toward me. We both held our gaze, standing only ten feet apart. After a head shake and a snort, the black approached a pace or two, extended its long snout and smelled me, then stepped closer and nuzzled my chest.

I fashioned a jaquima and reins from scraps of rope and cord in my pack. The black accepted the rig willingly. After hoisting my pack onto my back, I leaped aboard the back of the caballo and awaited his response. He bent his head around and smelled at my left boot. I heeled him gently, and together we proceeded down the trail.

For weeks I searched for Chávez with no luck. La gente told of Chávez visiting their pueblos, of preparing a meal for him. They told of his guerilla attacks on Mueller's vaqueros, often leaving more than one dead or dying. Then he would be gone.

Uncertain what to do, dreading the ghosts that waited for me there, I finally remembered the note I carried in my pocket and returned to Piedras Negras.

The pueblo had never recovered from the attack by the vaqueros. Only two of the casas had been rebuilt, but they had a look of impermanence, of transience, as if the residents were only waiting for the time to go elsewhere. Most of the homes were little more than burned-out rubble. It looked like most of la gente had moved away. I soon learned only three families remained to coax beans and squash from the soil. The doors were missing from the church, and goats wandered in and out of the sanctuary.

As I rode through the remains of the pueblo, an old man rose from where he was working on his knees at the edge of a field. I could not remember his name, but I recognized him as he strode toward me on aged legs. As he neared, I dismounted.

When he was still ten paces away he stopped, surprised, and peered at me.

I waved a greeting and said, "*Buenos días.* It is I, Carlos."

"*¡Válgame Dios!*" exclaimed the old man. He stepped forward and clasped my arms in his strong hands and stared into my face.

"*¡Válgame Dios!*" he repeated, and made the sign of the cross. "I thought you were Chávez, come to save us!"

Finally, he released his grip and said, "*Buenos días,* Carlos, how are you?"

"Very well, thank you. And you? Are you all right?"

"*Sí,* we are fine. No one has bothered us since . . ." He extended an arm toward the remnants of the village.

"How are Gustavo and Roberto?" I asked.

"Gustavo took his wife and children," he said, "loaded their few belongings onto a mule, and went to live with relatives far to the south. Roberto has work as a foreman for Señor Lucero, who owns a large rancho near Ciudad Chihuahua and is a breeder of horses. Señor Lucero's son is married to Roberto's cousin's daughter."

"Do you know where the rancho is? Can you tell me how to get there?"

"*Sí*, take the trail east to San Ysidro, then follow the well-traveled road to Guerrero, then to Cuauhtémoc. The road from Cuauhtémoc to Ciudad Chihuahua will pass by the rancho, which lies in the wide valley a few miles southwest of the city."

"*Gracias*. Can I do anything for you?"

"No, Carlos. Only prayers. You know you cannot stay here."

"*Sí*." I understood.

I scanned the horizon for a moment then said, "I'll just visit the campo santo, then go."

"No, Carlos. Do not go there."

"Why not?" I asked.

The old man shook his head, tears forming in his eyes. "It will not be good for you to go there," he said. "Please, just leave. Now."

I shook his hand and then embraced him briefly. Ignoring his request, I walked to the edge of the ruined village, tied the black to a low bush, and climbed the rocky hill that contained the cemetery.

Everything was destroyed. The lápidas had been knocked over, many of them broken. The graves had been violated, dug up, dark, empty eye sockets on the bare face of the hillside. It was as if someone had been searching for something. An ice-cold tremor racked my spine as I stood, shaking, in the bright warm sun.

I wandered through the devastated campo santo trying to locate María's grave. Everything was scattered, broken, half buried in rocks and debris. I was unable to recognize anything. A fire began growing within me as I clenched my jaws, fighting to remain calm.

I heard boots scraping on stone, and I turned to find the old man struggling up the hill toward me.

"Carlos, I tried to warn you," he said, laboring for breath.

"What happened? Who did this?" I asked through gritted teeth.

"Hacendado Mueller. He came himself. When his vaqueros did not return with you or proof of your death, when all they could report was that you were gone, he came to the village himself with his riders, his bodyguards."

The old man paused long enough to catch his breath. "Mueller questioned some of us about you, whether or not you were here, where you had gone. He held a gun to our heads."

He looked down the hill toward the ruined pueblo, then continued. "When we would not talk to him, he had his riders torture us, whip us. Still, we would not tell him anything."

Pointing toward the church, he said, "Mueller entered the *iglesia* and looked around and asked where the church money and gold chalices and cups had gone. When we told him that his own men stole them, he grew angry. He pulled *viejo* Gómez out of the crowd and shot him through the head."

Glancing around the campo santo, gesturing with his hands, the old man said, "Hacendado Mueller accused us of burying the church's objects and money here, in the cemetery. He ordered his riders to dig up the graves. Some of them even took the heads of young girls dead for years."

The old man paused, reluctant to go on. I encouraged him to tell me the rest.

"Hacendado Mueller was convinced we were hiding you. He tortured Gustavo and Roberto and others and from them learned about María and you. It was then that he ordered the campo santo destroyed."

I interrupted him with a wave of my hand. I had heard enough.

"Leave me alone, *por favor*."

"*Sí*, Carlos," he said. "I understand."

The Reunion

La Reunión

One week later, around midday, I arrived at the gate of Señor Lucero's rancho. Spotting two riders nearby, I spurred my black toward them. Both men eyed me warily as I approached, but relaxed as I waved a greeting and smiled.

"Where does foreman Roberto live?" I asked.

The men pointed to a well-kept, flat-roofed, freshly stuccoed adobe at the edge of a field of corn just to the west of the main hacienda. As I rode away, I could hear the two men whispering the name Chávez.

When I knocked on the door, a young woman cradling a baby answered. "*Buenas tardes,*" she said.

"*Buenas tardes,*" I returned, with a slight bow. "Does Roberto live here?"

"*Sí, señor,*" she said. "*Un momento.*"

She left the door open slightly and disappeared into the interior shadows. Seconds later, I heard the click of boot heels on the plank floor. Then Roberto was there, blinking at me in the sunlight with startled recognition. A large burn scar dominated the left side of his face, and his left ear was gone.

"Carlos? *¡Dios mio!* Is it you?"

I nodded my head and whispered, "Roberto."

We embraced and tears came, sudden and unbidden, to both of us.

Roberto led me inside and introduced me to the young woman. "My wife, Josefina." Pointing to the baby, he said, "My son, Crecencio."

Two bowls of posole were already set on the table. Josefina filled another, and Roberto invited me to sit and eat. As Josefina dined, she nursed the baby.

Pointing to Roberto's face and ear, I asked, "Mueller did this?"

"*Sí,*" he responded, setting his spoon in the bowl. "Gustavo is worse. They broke his hands so he cannot work. That is why he went to live with his uncle's family near Otero."

Tight-jawed, I said, "I just came from Piedras Negras."

Roberto placed his spoon on the table and looked down, fighting for composure.

"Mueller will pay," I said.

"No, Carlos," he said. "*Por favor.* It is over. Piedras Negras is no more. We must forget, we must go on from here. There is nothing we can do. We are too few, and we are armed with little more than axes and hoes with which to fight our enemies. We are too weak against Mueller and his vaqueros."

"You are wrong," I replied. "Something will be done. Even now, Chávez rides against the devil."

Roberto shook his head, then said to Josefina, "Leave us, *por favor.*"

Josefina hefted the baby against her shoulder and went outside. I watched out the window as she settled Crecencio in her shawl and began grooming a small, fenced garden plot.

Roberto spoke. "Señor Lucero, the man who owns this rancho, *mi jefe,* lost members of his family in Mueller's raids on Piedras Negras. He wanted to help rebuild the pueblo, but after what happened, few of *la gente* wished to remain. The ghosts are too many. He went to the officials, the *politicos,* the lawyers. He told them about hacendado Mueller, the raids, the rapes, the killings, but nothing was ever done. Joaquín Mueller's pockets run deep, and he even has relatives in the government."

Leaning across the table and lowering his voice, Roberto said, "Lucero hired mercenaries, *asesinos.* He said if the law would not exact justice, then he would see that it is done in his own way."

"What happened?" I asked.

"The *asesinos,* two of them, were sent back in whiskey barrels. Each had been horribly tortured with knives and fire before dying. Both were headless."

I sat silent for several minutes, then said, "I will take care of hacendado Mueller. It may be that I won't return either, but this must be done."

"No, Carlos. You cannot . . . "

"Yes, I can. And I will. And no one must know. Do you understand?"

Seeing my determination, Roberto relented. "*Sí,* Carlos, I understand. You will stay with us?"

"No. No one must know I was here, that we are amigos, or it could bad for you and your family if I don't succeed. Mueller's influence stretches far across the mountains and the llanos. I must leave now, but I will be back."

I got up from the table and went to the window, where I watched Josefina sitting on the edge of the porch, bouncing the baby on her leg. Roberto came to stand beside me. Seeing his wife and child, he smiled.

"Keep them safe," I said.

"I will, Carlos."

Following one final embrace, I went out into the day.

The Cave

La Cueva

The moment the sun dropped behind the ridge, the night carried an uneasy feeling. There was no moon. Low, dark clouds, thick with moisture condensed from the valley air, advected up the steep slope. Sinuous clusters of aerosol-light droplets floated through the trees and rocks, along the ground, and up to my hidden campsite on the mountainside.

Isolated, high above the nearest trail, I sat close to the fire, serape tight around my shoulders, hypnotized by the tongues of flame dancing with the burning branches and embers. I willed the warmth into my cold, aching body. I moved only to throw another dry stick into the blaze. At times, I heard my hobbled caballo grazing in the small clearing just beyond the crude camp, his hooves clicking against exposed granite. I leaned back on the saddle I employed as a pillow. The rifle leaned against the nearest tree, but the revolvers were still holstered and strapped around my hips.

The silence was broken only by the crackling fire and a rare leaf-rattling breeze. Though no sound triggered alertness, I sensed a presence, eyes staring at me from the forest.

I raised my eyes to a point just beyond the constricted illumination of the fire to the line of trees just beyond. The form of a man materialized, taking shape as swirls of mist parted like curtains. Hidden by the serape, my left hand inched toward a revolver. Another moment, and I recognized the Indian, his many-colored poncho hanging to his knees, its edges transitioning into the silver fog diverging and anastomosing along the ground. The firelight reflected the crucifix-shaped scar on his face and his coal black eyes burned.

Our stares held for several minutes. The Indian stood as if a statue.

"Are you apparition or dream?" I asked.

"Chávez needs you," he said, then turned and disappeared into the forest.

I stared into the blackness where he had vanished, his space filled with mist. An uncomfortable sensation urged me to saddle and bridle my horse and strap my gear behind the cantle. Mounted, I spurred the animal into the laurels where I had seen the Indian. Though little was visible in the darkness, the caballo surged forward as if he were being led. I gave him his head. The black never slackened his pace as we traveled into the thick woods, making our way among trees and rocks.

Hours later, the animal picked up his pace to a trot. The mist evaporated as we entered a narrow canyon. The clouds thinned and a hint of starlight penetrated. The caballo slowed again to a walk, then stopped, craning his large head forward, searching, sniffing the air. A horse whinnied in the distance.

Farther in the constricting canyon, a low fire set back in a deep shelter cave glowed. Without my urging, the black walked toward it. As we approached, five poncho-clad Indians appeared at the entrance standing rigid, blocking entry. A word from inside and they slipped silently into the forest.

I slid from the saddle, ground-hitched the black, and approached the opening. On each side of the entrance was a tall pile of rocks, large ones, placed there by men. I sensed they served as a kind of portal, a passage. A chill coursed down my spine as I advanced, not of fear but of apprehension. I felt as though I was trespassing on inviolable ground.

As I neared the entrance, the flickering firelight illuminated dark figures high on the cave walls, painted images of animals, some long extinct, and strange depictions of what I recognized as shamans, holy men. As the chill deepened, I realized this was a holy place, and had been for thousands of years. I felt rather than saw spirits moving at the edge of the light.

Barely illuminated beyond the fire, a man lay on a grass pallet, his hands crossed over his stomach. I stepped into the light holding my arms out to my sides, a gesture to show I was not holding a gun. The man's head lifted slightly.

"Carlos," rasped Chávez, with a weak grin. A wide bloodstain spread across the pallet beneath his torso, still damp. *Back shot,* I thought. The geography of the blood leakage could have resulted from nothing else.

I knelt beside the pallet.

"What can I do for you?" I asked.

"There is nothing you can do, *compa.* My *hermanos* have cared for me since I received the wound yesterday. They know what to do."

I stared at the blood-soaked margin of his camisa. "Did Mueller do this?"

"*Sí.* A bullet from the hacendado. I was alone, watering Pesadilla at the Río Pardo, when I was ambushed. I took out three vaqueros but ran out of luck. I barely escaped. I don't think Mueller knows he hit me."

Great pain pounded his eyes. He squeezed them shut and paused for several breaths, trying to regain his composure.

"I have run out of time," he said.

I placed my fingers on his neck. The pulse was weak, erratic.

"Chávez . . ." I started.

Chávez tried to raise his hand to stop me, but only his fingers moved.

"Let me speak," he said. "I don't wonder why you are here, why you came to this place, to the sierras. I am convinced you were delivered to us, to help us fight. You have done more than was ever asked of you. I grieve for your loss at Piedras Negras. I, more than anyone, know how much you lost there."

A seizure of coughing racked his body. Another minute passed as he tried to regain his breath.

"You see a dying man before you, but I tell you, Carlos, I am more fortunate than you. You do not need to worry. I am going to meet my family. At last, we will be together. It is where I need to be; I know that."

He fought for more air.

"Carlos, you have not discovered yet where you need to be. You search, thinking you will find it here, in Mexico. I remember those days when I, too, reveled in the search, the quest. But the answer does not lie in these mountains, canyons, forests. It lies deep within your heart. It is there, and only there, that you will find what you are looking for. And you must ask yourself this question: Is this still your fight?"

"Chávez, I . . ."

"Do not speak now. I must rest."

His head sagged to the pallet. I sat beside him as he fell into a restless, troubled sleep.

I remained near him until I could no longer sit upright. Weary, I moved over to the far wall of the cave, leaned back, and slept.

• • •

I awoke with a jerk. My left hand groped for my revolver. Predawn light diffused into the cave.

Chilled, I looked over at the fire and it was out. I rose to gather fuel and saw that Chávez was gone. I peered out of the entrance into the dim light but saw nothing, no one. Near my feet on the rock floor of the cave two drops of blood glistened.

I walked out and searched the adjacent canyon and saw no sign save for the footprints of the indios from the night before. I heard no sound except that of a caballo snorting: Pesadilla, grazing on the grasses growing near the tiny stream, my own black feeding several yards beyond.

Through scattered clouds the sun broke over the eastern rim of the canyon. I walked back to the cave, boots wet with morning dew. Inside, I knelt next to the empty, bloodstained pallet. It did not seem possible to me that Chávez could be dead.

Chávez's belongings were stacked against the wall of the cave—belt, holsters, revolvers, bandoleras, rifle, boots, boxes of ammunition, and sombrero. Nearby were his saddle, blankets, and bridle.

• • •

I rekindled the fire and heated tortillas on a rock. After eating I donned Chávez's gear, cleaned and loaded the weapons, and saddled and bridled Pesadilla. I rode out of the canyon in the direction of Mueller's rancho, leaving my black behind. I felt the horse's muscles ripple under me, felt a surge of energy, of power. I felt strong. I thought of Chávez's last words to me: *Is this still your fight?* I spurred Pesadilla into a lope.

For a week I rode, stopping only for water and food. As I passed though the pueblos, la gente stared at Pesadilla, at me. I heard them whisper, *Chávez, Chávez*. Some ran to me to touch my leg, to warn that the vaqueros still searched.

I traveled the main roads with the hope that the vaqueros would find me. Death no longer mattered. Death, for me, had lost its authenticity.

The Justice
La Justicia

Three hours past sundown one week later, I stood on the low ridge looking down on the vaqueros' cabins, the same one from which I had witnessed the killing of El Enano. Thin clouds drifted across a high half-moon as I watched the cabin lights extinguished one by one.

I stood silent and unmoving for another hour, giving the members of the households time to reach a deep slumber before I set out, giving myself time to prepare, to find my center, as Chávez taught me. While I waited, I looked across the plain at hacendado Mueller's fortressed hacienda a mile beyond the tiny community of vaqueros. In the distance I could just make out light coming from windows.

I mounted Pesadilla, rode along the ridge for two hundred yards, then descended into the expansive valley, keeping wide of the vaquero settlement so as not to alert their dogs. My cuchillo dangled from the thong around my neck.

As I traveled across the flat, open ground, I remained alert for riders or guards, but saw none. Thirty minutes later, I halted in a small copse of trees near a stream, dismounted, and ground-hitched Pesadilla. I removed the belt containing the holstered guns and hung it across the saddle horn. Taking only the cuchillo, I struck out on foot across the remaining distance to the walled enclosure.

Before another fifteen minutes passed, I was standing next to the eight-foot-high enclosure that surrounded Mueller's hacienda and grounds. Constructed of rock and adobe, the wall was three-feet thick.

My movement near the entrance, closed by a locked iron gate, elicited a response from two large German shepherds that leaped from the shadows, snarling. Trailing the dogs was a pair of guards, each carrying a rifle. Keeping close to the wall, I sprinted to the rear of the compound.

When I made it to the rear of the walled grounds, I reached up, my fingers searching for and finding a hold on the rim. Pulling myself up, I squatted atop the massive fence and surveyed the vast, manicured grounds, looking for a place of concealment. I spotted a pair of pecan trees one hundred feet away.

Before the guards completed their evaluation of the disturbance near the front gate, I dropped onto the grass, sprinted to the nearest pecan tree, and pulled myself up into the lower branches. Scurrying along a thick limb, I leaped out into the narrow void between the two trees, found a hold on a branch from the second, and clambered to a hiding place some twenty feet above the ground. I wedged myself into a crotch such that I would be hard to see from the ground.

Within minutes, the guards came into view. When the dogs crossed my trail, they started snuffling and whining. The men, alerted, unhooked the leashes and encouraged them to follow the scent.

The shepherds sniffed for several seconds, then followed my scent to the base of the first tree. Heads raised toward the upper reaches of the tree, the dogs growled and barked. The guards circled, straining to see into the dense network of branches.

Finally, one of the men lowered his rifle and said, "*Hay nada.*" It is nothing.

As a guard called to the dogs—Diablo and El Rey—their attention was directed to a movement at the base of the wall. As I watched from my place of concealment, the shepherds dashed toward the wall, renewing their barking. The guards, rifles pointing, followed.

A raccoon, caught at his nightly prowling, had assumed a defensive position on his hind legs, front claws extended, hissing at the dogs.

The shepherds paused only long enough to get a whiff of the intruder, then tore into it as the guards watched. Seconds later, Diablo, gripping the lifeless raccoon in his jaws, tossed it about as a cat does a rat. After another minute, the shepherds had grown tired of the sport and sat, licking the blood from their paws.

The guards, relieved to discover the intruder was only a raccoon, laughed and lowered their rifles. They whistled for the dogs, leashed them, and led them back in the direction from which they had come.

When they neared the house, a tall, rangy figure stepped from the shadows with a revolver in his hand. As he entered the stream of light from an uncurtained window, I noticed handsome, sharply chiseled features and a well-groomed moustache.

"*¿Qué pasa?*" the man asked.

"It is nothing, Señor Mueller," replied one of the guards. "Only a raccoon. Diablo and El Rey killed it, over there."

Mueller peered in the direction to which the guard pointed. "*Bueno,*" he said. "But remain vigilant. I have a bad feeling."

"*Sí,* Señor Mueller." The two guards spoke in unison.

Mueller executed a military-style about-face and vanished around the corner of the house. A moment later I heard a door close.

I waited in the tree for another thirty minutes. Dropping to the ground, I sprinted to the corner of the casa where Mueller and the guards had conversed. Bolted to the wall here was a six-foot-wide wrought-iron trellis. Flowering vines twisted upward toward the second story.

Taking a deep breath and making no sound, I looked around the corner. I found a recessed patio, at the far end of which was a door that entered the casa.

Reclining in front of the door was one of the German shepherds.

I stepped backward out of sight. Leaning against the wall, I fought to control my breathing. As I waited for my pulse to return to normal, I removed my cuchillo from the scabbard. A minute passed. Then two. A deep breath, a silent prayer, and I stepped out.

Shoulders squared, feet set wide apart, I held the knife in my left hand, and whispered, "Diablo!"

The dog's ears pricked; his head shot up. He leaped to his feet, his canine eyes searching the shadows for the source of the sound.

He found me.

Growling, he lowered his large head, and, roaching the fur along the back of his neck, he loped toward me, gaining speed with every step. Eight feet away, the shepherd snarled and leaped, snapping jaws aimed for my throat.

I shot my right hand up under the deadly muzzle, seizing the dog in a tight grip by its thick neck. With my left hand I plunged the knife into its right side up to the hilt. The impact from the weight and momentum of the heavy shepherd knocked me backward and to the ground, the dog landing on top of me. As I held the frothing mouth away from my throat, I stabbed repeatedly with the knife, fairly tearing a hole in the right side of the animal. The shepherd's hind legs raked my thighs while its blood drained onto my clothes and the ground. With a shudder and expelling of foul air, the shepherd died.

I shoved the dog off of me, rose, and replaced the cuchillo in the scabbard. A second later, I heard the rapidly approaching barking of the second dog. Looking around for someplace to hide, I spotted the trellis, climbed to the top, and clung to a rail.

The surviving shepherd, alerted by the earlier sounds of his now dead brother, bounded into view, leash trailing. Spotting the dead dog, he approached cautiously, circling the body, extending his long nose, separating the scents. When El Rey reached a position beneath me, I released my hold on the rail and launched myself from the trellis.

I landed on the shepherd's back, slamming my boots into his spine with all the strength I could summon. Injured, stunned, and breathless, the dog squirmed under me. I reached for the leash, wrapped it around the thick neck, and strangled him.

I jumped to my feet, withdrawing the cuchillo, and awaited the arrival of the guards. None appeared, so I went searching for them.

I located one of the sentries seated on a bench smoking a cigarette, his rifle resting against the bole of an adjacent tree. A revolver resided in a belt holster. Either he did not hear the earlier barking of the dogs or was unconcerned, believing perhaps they had found another raccoon. I looked around for the second guard but saw no one.

Finishing his cigarette, the sentry rose, stretched, and yawned. He glanced toward the house, then sat on the ground with his back against the tree trunk next to the rifle. After getting comfortable, he lowered his head on his chest. I waited. Ten minutes later I was rewarded by the sound of his light snoring.

Silent on the soft grass, I crept up behind the guard. I slipped the revolver from his holster and placed it behind the tree. I picked up the rifle next to him and placed the tip of the cold barrel against his forehead, nudging him awake.

The guard stared in disbelief and made a sudden grab for his revolver. Finding it gone, he shrugged in resignation, and leaned back against the tree.

"If you want to live," I said, "you will answer my questions. If I find you are lying, I will slit your throat."

He nodded.

"The other guard?" I asked.

Taking a deep breath, he said, "His shift was over." He pointed in the direction of the vaquero cabins and said, "He went home. Another will arrive at dawn to relieve me."

Gesturing toward a lighted window on the second floor, I asked, "Mueller?"

"*Sí.* He is probably in the bedroom or his library, both on the second floor. He often works late at night."

"Is he alone?"

"*Sí.* His wife is in Mexico City with relatives, I think."

"Are there dogs in the house?"

"No."

"Remove your boots and pants."

I ordered the guard to tear his pantalones into strips. With these I bound his wrists and legs, stuffed his socks into his mouth, fastened a gag, and dragged him into the shrubs.

• • •

At the patio door I paused and listened. Hearing nothing, I tried the latch but it was locked. Slipping my knife from the scabbard, I inserted it between the door and the jamb and pried the bolt back.

I stepped into a large sitting room furnished with leather chairs and couch and polished tables. Along one wall was a mahogany bookcase. In the moonlight that filtered through the windows, I could see the titles of classic Mexican and American literature. I replaced the knife in the scabbard.

The stairs to the second story, like the floor of the room I had just quit, were stone tile, and my boots made no sound as I took them one by one.

At the head of the stairs I saw light spilling out of an open door. Taking short, silent steps and stopping often to listen, I made my way toward it.

Stopping in the doorway of the library, I spotted Mueller seated at a dark cherry wood desk that faced the entrance to the room, his attention directed toward several sheets of paper spread out before him. He held a pen in his right hand and from time to time marked something on one of the documents. At his right elbow was the revolver he carried earlier, a .38 caliber.

I stepped into the room and stood some eight feet in front of his desk.

Mueller made another mark with his pen. Without looking up, he said, "You might as well step closer so I can see you."

I needed to close the distance. I took two long steps forward and halted, my arms hanging loose at my sides. I was now three feet from the desk.

Mueller raised his eyes, regarding me. His stare lingered on my blood-soaked pantalones and camisa. I imagined him wondering if the blood was from his guards. He glanced down at the revolver, sat back in his chair, and folded his hands across his lap.

"Ah," he said. "The gringo. For a moment I feared you might be Chávez."

I said nothing.

"We have not heard anything about you in a year. Some of my men said you were probably dead. Others said you simply went away after Piedras Negras."

At the mention of the pueblo I stiffened, jaw tightening. Mueller noticed.

"I knew some day you would come," he said.

Imperceptibly, I moved toward the desk, scant fractions of an inch at a time.

"I learned about you and the young lady in Piedras Negras," he said. "One of the villagers explained the details of your relationship while I pressed my revolver into his cheek."

Another inch.

"Touching, your affections for one another. At that point I realized that since I could never find you to capture or to kill, I might convince you to come looking for me. I believed it was just a matter of time before you found out about the cemetery, about how we dug up María's body."

Mueller was trying to break me, to distract me. He was toying with me, the game bringing him pleasure. He looked into my eyes and saw he was getting to me.

Another inch.

"And now," he said, "here you are, delivering yourself up to me." He grinned, perfect teeth sparkling in the light of the room.

Another inch.

Shifting his weight in the chair, Mueller asked, "How did you get past my guards? The dogs? *Pues*, no matter. You are here now."

He placed his elbows on the desk and leaned his chin on folded hands.

"Chávez has cost me many men, much livestock," he said. "Because of him, the campesinos are not easy to displace. He gives them hope, and because they have hope, they fight."

Closer.

"You are almost as bad as Chávez, almost as much trouble. The campesinos regard you as a hero, the gringo who considers their fight worthy. Did you know the campesinos sing *cantos* about you and Chávez?"

Almost there.

Leaning back into his plush chair again, Mueller said, "You were foolish to come here, no?"

I moved again, my final step placing me just in front of his desk.

At that moment, it dawned on Mueller that I had reduced the distance between the two of us. He raised up in his chair and shot his right hand toward the revolver.

It was just enough time for me to draw the cuchillo. As Mueller's fingers tightened around the butt of the .38, I slammed the knife down and through his wrist, impaling it to the desk. His fingers hovered over the revolver, unable to close. I picked it from the desk and threw it into the hallway.

Mueller's mouth opened and closed, emitting a high-pitched whine of pain. Spittle bubbled from his lips, anger at this turn of events exploding from his eyes. I came behind the desk, seized him by the throat, and lifted him from the chair, his arm still held fast by the blade. As I did with the German shepherd, I tightened the grip, calling into play muscle that had been honed fighting and working these past months, muscles prepared for this moment.

My fingernails cut into the flesh of his neck as I closed the grip tighter, tighter, shutting off all sound, all air.

The hacendado sagged, quivered, only seconds away from dying of strangulation. Releasing my grip, I jerked the knife away, freeing his wrist, and he fell to the floor, gasping for air, painful sounds coming from his crushed throat.

Stepping behind him, I grabbed Joaquín Mueller by the hair and pulled his head back so he could look up and into my eyes. I raised the cuchillo and some of the blood it had drawn from his wrist dripped onto his face.

Mueller tried to speak but no words came from his ruined throat.

I forced my eyes away from his and stared at my knife, turning it over once, twice. I returned my gaze to Mueller, but he, too, was looking at the cuchillo.

I waited until I was certain he knew what was going to happen to him.

The Meeting

La Sesión

Two months after leaving the Mueller rancho, I arrived at the casa of Roberto and Josefina. Seated at the kitchen table and sipping coffee, Roberto and I made small talk for several minutes.

When Josefina left to go work in her garden, Roberto turned to me and said, "We have heard tales from the countryside. I only know bits and pieces."

I said nothing.

Silence reigned for a full minute, broken only by the muted clinking of Roberto's spoon as he stirred sugar into his coffee.

"*La gente* are moving back to Piedras Negras," he said.

I nodded. More silence.

"*Mi jefe*, Señor Lucero, would like a meeting with you."

• • •

Midmorning of the following day, an impeccably dressed maid led me to an elegant drawing room in the main ranch house where I waited a few minutes before Lucero arrived. He was dressed in a white linen shirt, khaki pants, and European leather sandals. After offering me a drink and exchanging a few pleasantries, he grew serious.

"Roberto has told me about you," he said. "I will skip the formalities and get right to the point. I will pay you ten thousand pesos if you will hand it over to me."

As he waited for my reply, he poured another splash of expensive tequila into my glass.

"What gives you reason to think I know of what you speak?" I asked. I felt the weight of my knife hanging from my neck inside my camisa.

Lucero leaned back in his leather chair, took a deep breath, then said, "The campesinos bring us rumors about the bizarre killing of hacendado Mueller."

"Tell me what you have heard," I said.

"Mueller's body was found by one of his guards just after sunup one morning two months ago. He had been wired to an iron trellis near his patio in the manner of a crucifixion, if you will, but upside down."

Lucero waited for a response, a sign. He got nothing.

Lucero leaned forward, his eyes seeking mine. We locked stares. "His head was missing," he said.

I moved not a muscle nor blinked.

"His blood had drained out of him to puddle around the carcass of a dead German shepherd, one of his guard dogs."

The tequila was smooth, well aged, and the limes were sweet, the best I'd ever tasted. The room drew in on us while the fan above our heads squeaked birdlike as it pushed air gently about.

When I said nothing, offered no reaction, Lucero continued. "It is said you have it. It is said by Mueller's own vaqueros that it was you who had been to the rancho, to the *hacienda grande*. It is said you slipped by them all."

I sipped the remaining tequila, taking a long suck on the lime. I looked out the broad, tinted, second story window at the rich pastures below, at a herd of thoroughbreds prancing along a fence line in the distance. I searched the yard at the low adobe by the cornfield and spotted Josefina hoeing weeds away from some small plants.

Growing emphatic, Lucero said, "It is the most important thing in my life. I must have it for myself, for my people. I want to take it to Piedras Negras and the other pueblos. I want it to serve as a reminder, to show *la gente* that we prevailed, that we can rebuild, that peace will return to us. It is something the Indians, the Mexicans can understand."

"I will think about it," I said. I set my empty glass on the polished teak wood bar and stood.

Lucero rose, shook my hand, and we parted, he to his herds and I to a nearby village where I was renting a room.

That evening I sat in the cantina and listened as the guitarrista played "El Cascabel." He coaxed melodies woven of love and violence from the gut strings of the delicate, homemade instrument. As the cantos seeped through the low-ceilinged room, I sipped more tequila and thought about the ten thousand pesos.

I thought about the man Lucero hated. I thought about my friends who were dead because of him. I thought about the women raped, shared among his vaqueros, then left to die at the side of the road. I thought about the hangings, the killing of the children, the destruction of villages. I thought about the way he must have smiled as he manipulated men to kill for him, all because he wanted land that belonged to others.

As the music moved around the room, moving gently into every corner, I barely heard it as I became lost in thoughts, feelings. Cloudy images of El Enano, Herrera, Tomasito, and the others passed before my eyes.

I took another sip of the tequila, realizing I probably had too much. I pushed the glass away, thinking if I removed the drink, I would rid myself of the images.

The music played on, the room grew darker, the clouds formed again before me and, suddenly, there was María, reaching out for me.

• • •

The *cantinero* shook me gently, saying it was time to close. I looked around, saw chairs stacked on tables, an old, white-haired man mopping the tile floor, the band, with their instruments, walking out the front door.

I rubbed my eyes with closed fists and discovered I had been crying.

• • •

That night in my room, I sat on the bed for hours. The tears returned and I did not fight them. I let them flow, soaking my shirt. In an odd way, it felt good to cry, to release all that had remained trapped deep within. Black tears of hate and anger. Tears of loss.

I slid my hand under my camisa to the knife that hung on my chest. I thought for a moment about the look on Mueller's face during the last seconds of his life.

No, I would not deliver it to Lucero, never. Not for ten thousand pesos, not for anything.

The hacendado's head would remain where it had been for the past two months. With me.

Epilogue

Praying for Storms

Ex-combatant, relearning human laws
you'll cleanse the taint,
Your scarred or calloused hand
remembering gentleness, restraint.

—Alfred Corn

Two or three times each year I return to Mexico. I find I cannot live without the replenishment offered by her deserts, her mountains. I go to escape, to sweat city poisons from my blood, to purge the growing bitter taste of what men call progress and civilization from my mind, to remove myself from the superficial worlds of money and society and its many facades. I go to refresh, rejuvenate, reassess. I search the desert for the right path. I roam the mountains in search of peace and balance. Each time I go I find, and incorporate, more strength.

In the waking sleep of the Mexican desert stone and sand, among the brush and sparse trees, among the rabbit and coyote, in the wake of the flight of eagle and crow, below the vast sky and infinite horizon where I hear only the voice of the wind, see only the arc of the sun, I find truth, find my true self and rejoice.

My days are filled with the taste and smell of the outdoors, of earth tones, large trees, large mountains, large dreams. My days are filled with shades of blue, sky colors, and gentle, soft things, coupled with bright reveries.

But, when the nights come, I pray for storms so that the dark clouds will hide the stars. Sometimes, when the memories and the dreams come flooding back, fast, furious, without mercy, without respite, I lose myself in drink so I won't have to think about guns and knives and how they were used, about the overriding fear, the horror of what I saw. About what I did.

I cannot fight the dreams. I am helpless in their arms.

In that faraway place in that faraway time, Mexico was many things to me. She offered me a place when I felt I had none. She provided passion when I thought mine was lost. She furnished adventure whether I wished it or not. She opened her horizons to me, embraced me, held on to me for a long time, then, when I was ready, she let me go.

The ideals of the lowly campesinos burned like a hot brand on my consciousness, roared like an out-of-control prairie fire, growing hotter, brighter, moving fast, deadly, taking everything in its path.

The flow of the revolution, the fight for the land, for dignity, for peace, for freedom, swept past me like floodwaters surging, ripping, unstoppable, carrying me along.

Wrongs were sometimes righted, sometimes not. In the process of trying to right wrongs, others were committed. By the leaders. By us.

By me.

Life was precious and at the same time cheap. It came and went. We could not stop. We could not stop riding and fighting. It was the only thing we knew to do.

Years ago I heard a call from the other side of the border, and I answered it. Enough time has passed that it should be easy to forget, but some stains can never be removed. Like the stars in the heavens, they never go away. Sometimes, they will cloud over, but the clouds never last.

That's why I pray for storms.

Acknowledgments

Every book is a collaborative effort. I was fortunate to land in a situation where I worked with talented, energetic, and professional people. *Muchas gracias* to Luther Wilson, who provided opportunities and encouragement; to Judy Wilson, who fed me, gave me a place to stay when I drifted into town, and provided great conversation and company; to Maya Allen-Gallegos for her astute editorial eye; to the entire University of New Mexico Press family, who seem to have a lot of fun making great books. Thanks to agent Cherry Weiner for her advice and belief in me.

Deep gratitude is due to one of the best vision editors in the country, Laurie Wagner Buyer. She patiently took a nervous and intimidated writer with some old poems and a story, added her creative genius, and guided me on the journey to a finished book.

Finally, I owe so much, including my life, to the men I rode with in Mexico. They befriended a lost and wandering gringo youth and shared what they had: a little food, a campsite, a powerful sense of justice, important survival skills, and a new way of looking at the world. Though decades have passed, not a day goes by that I do not think of them.